DORIAN ROCKWOOD

THE CASH CACHE MYSTERY

THE CASH CACHE MYSTERY

For information contact:

Insundry Productions Books

Gardnerville NV 89460

insundryproductions.com

Cover illustration by Duy Phan

ISBN (ebook): 978-1-962056-01-4

ISBN (paperback): 978-1-962056-00-7

Library of Congress Control Number: 2023913631

Also by Dorian Rockwood

Treachery Unmasked

Chapter One

The war surplus jeep swung out of the dirt road and accelerated down the two-lane highway, seventeen-year-old Dan Case at the wheel. His brother Paul reached back and steadied the fishing rods.

"Make sure my sketchbook doesn't blow out," Dan shouted over the four-cylinder engine's noise and wind roaring through the open vehicle.

"It's okay." Paul turned forward, grabbing the passenger seat arm to steady himself. "It's under the tackle box."

Dan nodded a reply and shifted to third gear. The jeep bounced and hopped down the road, the chassis clanging as if every piece of metal inside was striking another. Dan held onto the wheel not only to steer, but in order to keep from being tossed out. The pair drove in silence, each accustomed to the loud noise after owning the vehicle for a year. They avoided lengthy conversation altogether when they rode in it. If they tried, they ended up yelling so much they became hoarse.

A late model blue sedan zoomed past them, its engine rumbling.

"Nice car." Paul checked over his shoulder before leaning toward

Dan. "Now a Greyhound is coming up behind us."

"I'm already doing 45!" Dan shouted back. "Can't go any faster in this thing. If it wants to pass me, let him go. I'm not arguing with a bus."

Dan pulled over to the right as far as he could. The huge bus roared past. Both brothers winced and turned their heads away as the Greyhound blew its horn and a blast of air hit them as it passed. The bus returned to the lane, belching a burst of black diesel exhaust. The billowing smoke clung to their clothes and hair as they whipped through the cloud.

"I bet they do that on purpose!" Paul coughed and fanned one hand in front of his face to clear the lingering black smoke. "The driver must push a button on the dash!"

Dan laughed as Paul braced his feet against the floor and pulled off his glasses, cleaning them with the bottom of his tee-shirt. Dan checked the dashboard.

"We need some gas," he called to his brother. "How much do you have on you?"

"About half a dollar, I think." Paul slipped his glasses back on.

"Maybe I've got a quarter," Dan said. "That will get us about four gallons."

The highway cut through a hillside forest. The trees, mighty oaks and maples, grew so thick that the woods were almost impenetrable. Scattered between the forests, on either side of the pavement, lay small family farms, many of them still tended by the descendants of the original nineteenth-century settlers, growing corn and hay and raising dairy cows, pigs, chickens and sheep.

The Wayside Filling Station came into view as the jeep rounded a curve. The Greyhound stood next to it, its door open. Some of the passengers milled around, stretching their legs.

"That story of the tortoise and the hare is correct!" Dan pointed at the bus. "Slow and steady wins the race! Or at least comes in a strong second." He turned into the driveway, the signal bell clanging as he stopped by the pumps. He glanced at the prices on the sign. "Damn! Look at that! Twenty-three cents a gallon now!" He reached in his pocket, pulled out some coins, then held out his hand. "Put some money in the pot, son."

Another teen came out of the garage, wearing blue coveralls with a "Ken" name patch sewn on and wiping his hands with an oily rag that was probably red once. He grinned as he approached the jeep. "Hey! It's the Bobbsey Twins!"

"Bobbsey Twins," Paul grumbled as he fished out his money and slapped the coins in Dan's outstretched palm.

Dan spoke out of the corner of his mouth. "Down, killer, down."

Ken stopped next to Dan, one hand resting on the top of the windshield while the other gripped the rear of the open doorway. He titled his head toward the fishing gear. "Any luck?"

"Caught our limit of trout," Dan waved at the creel holding the catch. "We went to the north end of the lake."

"I'll have to try out there." Ken stood at attention and saluted. "What will it be, sir? Fill it up with super? Our super is the finest grade of gasoline money can buy. The best super I reckon for 1947." He lowered his voice and nodded at the office. "We're supposed to say that to every customer. At least when the boss is around."

Dan grinned. "And very well done, I must say. But our jeep wouldn't know what to do with high grade gas. It would probably get drunk. Give us..." he counted up his handful of coins, "...seventy-two cents of regular."

"Coming up." Ken walked to the pump, then quickly came back to the driver's side. It didn't take long to put in less than three gallons. Dan dropped the coins into Ken's hand. "Thanks. Want the windshield cleaned?"

Dan responded in a poor imitation of an English accent. "That will not be necessary, kind sir." He indicated his brother. "My man here will take care of that when we put the Rolls into the garage."

"If I don't do it all right and proper like," Paul added, "he beats me with a stick."

Ken laughed. "Likely story. How's the next Joe Louis doing?"

"My dear brother, the Brunette Bomber," Dan grinned.

"Won my last bout," Paul gave a thumbs up. "The other guy never laid a glove on me. At least, no more than twice. Maybe the driver of that exhaust-puking Greyhound would like a match. Say, why is it still here?"

Ken glanced at the bus. "Oh, this is now supposed to be some kind of rest stop. The boss is talking about putting in a hot dog stand or pay toilets or something to rake in some extra dough. By the way, you may need some air in your left rear tire. It looks a little low. We fixed our pump finally."

Dan looked where Ken pointed. "Thanks. We'll just fill it up here."

"Well, back to the oil change job," Ken waved. "See ya!"

"Yeah, see ya!" the brothers said in unison.

Ken shook his head and chuckled as he started back toward the garage. "See? Just like the Bobbsey—"

Dan hit the button to turn on the engine, drowning out the rest of the sentence. The Greyhound's driver called all the passengers back. The door closed with a hiss and with a growling exhalation of more exhaust, the bus continued its journey through the countryside toward town.

"Paul, look, I know that the Bobbsey Twins thing bothers you," Dan said to his brother as they parked next to the air pump, "but Ken's a good guy. He's just trying to be funny."

"I know, but we've been hearing that same crack since elementary school," Paul complained. "I mean, it's getting old. Like we don't know we're identical twins?" He gave an irritated sigh. "Besides, it's not even accurate. The Bobbsey Twins were a boy and a girl, not identical. Nan and Bert, Freddie and Flossie."

"How do you know that?"

"I went to the library and looked it up years ago. I'll check the oil." Paul climbed out, went to the front, and lifted the hood.

Dan hopped out of the jeep and grabbed the hose, pulling it to the left rear wheel. He squatted on the ground and unscrewed the valve cap. After squirting some air in the tire, he got up and turned around. He jumped a little.

A tall, thin man stood behind him. The suit he wore appeared new, but not particularly expensive, and hung on him as if it was still on its hanger.

For a second, the man seemed to recognize Dan, then he gave a wan smile. "Forgive me. I didn't mean to startle you."

"That's all right." Dan reeled in the hose, then brushed off his hands. "I just didn't hear you."

"I've been told I have a light tread."

"You can say that again," Dan said.

Paul slammed down the hood and walked next to Dan. "Oil's fine."

The man glanced between the two. He audibly gasped.

"You're not seeing double," Dan assured him. "We're twins."

"Except I'm the more handsome one," Paul tapped himself on his chest.

"Says you," Dan shot back.

"Oh, good." The man seemed relieved. "You see, I've been sick. I've been in the hospital for months."

The siblings exchanged glances. There was something pathetic about him; his pallor looked as if he hadn't been in the sun in years.

"That's too bad," said Paul. "Are you better now?"

"Yes, a lot." The man brightened. "You see, I'm on my way to my brother's place in Omaha, Nebraska. He has a small business there and has offered me a job."

"Oh, that's great. Did you miss the Greyhound?" Dan jerked his thumb in the direction the bus took. "Didn't get back on time from the rest stop?"

"No, I wasn't on the bus," the man said. "The doctor suggested I get plenty of fresh air, so I thought I might try hitchhiking to get to Nebraska. I might get strong enough to help to my brother when I arrive."

"That sounds like a great idea." Dan spoke with a little too much enthusiasm, partly to cover his own discomfort over the man's situation. "Doesn't it, Paul?"

As sometimes happens between them, Dan didn't have to ask the next question. He looked at Paul, and his brother nodded.

"If you decide not to hitchhike any longer, we'd be glad to take you as far as Farmingford," Dan said. "We live there ourselves. It's a small town, but the bus stops right in front of the drug store. I'm afraid you'll have to stay overnight, since that was today's last northbound Greyhound."

"That's kind of you," the man said. "But I don't want to put you to any trouble."

"It's not any trouble at all," Dan patted the hood. "Although we need to let you know in all fairness, you'll be hitching a lift in a 1945 ex-army jeep. It's quite a different experience, but you probably rode in one during the war."

"Oh, I didn't serve in the military," the man sounded slightly ashamed. "My health, you know."

"Yes, of course," Dan flushed a little in embarrassment at his oversight.

"Do you mind hanging on to the fishing rods?" Paul tilted the driver's seat forward. "They won't go anywhere else. Just give me the other things. They can go in the back. Your suitcase should fit next to you."

The man handed the tackle box to Paul, then picked up the

sketchbook. "Who does the drawing?"

"Artist here." Dan raised his hand, then pointed to Paul. "Athlete there."

"May I look?" The man tentatively tapped the cover.

"Absolutely," Dan grinned.

"He loves it when people gush over his art." Paul stowed the tackle box.

"Just like he eats up the cheering crowds at boxing matches," Dan retorted.

The man leafed through the pages. "These are excellent. Very colorful landscapes."

"Thank you," Dan beamed. "I sell them at the local historical society gift store."

"And he gives trading stamps with every purchase," Paul added.

Dan titled his head toward his brother. "The extra ones I paste over his mouth."

The man flashed a quiet smile. "This one of the boxer...you, I suppose?" he looked at Paul, who nodded, "... is quite dynamic. A striking likeness."

"Of course, he had an exceptional model," Paul put in. Dan rolled his eyes.

"Where's this?" The man held the book open to a page.

"That?" Dan peered at the drawing. "Oh, that's what remains of Wolf Lodge, out by the lake."

"Remains?" A look of concern flashed over the man's face.

Dan got behind the wheel. "A fire happened there a few years ago. The interior was heavily damaged...almost gutted."

"Oh." The man returned the book to Paul, then climbed in the back. Paul started to slide the sketchbook under the tackle box. "No need to do that. I'll hold it in my lap."

"Thanks." Paul handed the sketchbook back and got into the passenger seat. "Dan, drop me off at the Epsteins, will you? It's their day."

"Paul has cornered the lawn mowing business in town," Dan told their rider. "He knows every blade of grass personally."

"I get to be outside," said Paul, "and at least I'm not a jerk."

"I work behind the lunch counter at the Allen Drug Store," Dan said. "He means 'soda jerk'."

Paul folded his arms. "Not necessarily."

Dan slugged his brother in the arm. "No more free sodas for you, bub." He started the engine and called over his shoulder. "Remember, we warned you!"

The jeep pulled out of the gas station and returned to the highway. A few minutes later, Dan saw a black delivery truck coming up behind them. He muttered angrily.

"What?" asked Paul.

"That guy back there is on my bumper," Dan yelled back irritably. "I wish he'd pass!" He stuck out his left hand and tried to wave the other driver past.

The truck finally passed them, and as he did, the man at the wheel honked his horn and waved. Dan noticed in the rear-view mirror that their passenger was looking away from the truck.

"Idiot!" Dan said under his breath as the truck pulled ahead. "Recognize it, Paul?"

His brother shook his head. "Not a local one."

They drove on until reaching the outskirts of Farmingford. The highway turned into the town's main street, lined with stores and businesses. They drove by the post office and a daycare center next to the local library branch. The church stood by the town hall, a brick building with columns in front and a clock over the doors. Dan turned into a residential street, tidy, small bungalows huddled along the curb. The trees were large and old and gave the residents welcome places to escape from their homes when it grew too hot.

After they stopped in front of a green cottage, Paul hopped out of the jeep. He turned to their rider. "Good luck at your new job."

"My new—oh yes, thank you." The man smiled.

"I'm closing tonight, so I'll eat at work," Dan said to Paul. "I'll put one of the trout in the refrigerator for you."

"Thanks!" Paul waved and walked toward the Epstein's detached garage.

"Climb up here." Dan motioned to his passenger. "It's a little more comfortable—but not much."

"Oh, yes, certainly." The man switched to the front seat.

"Watch this." Dan nudged the man and nodded at his brother. "Right on time. See the window in the white house next door? The curtain just pulled back a little? That's Betty Wilson peeking out. She's a cheerleader at school. In about an hour, she'll bring Paul a tall glass of ice cold lemonade. It's like a mating dance between a couple of birds." He heaved an exaggerated sigh. "Why do the girls go for the brutish athletes, and not for the sensitive artiste?" He laughed. "Where do you want to be dropped?"

"When does the next bus come through town? Do you know?"

"There are two in the morning, going north and south," Paul said.

"And you said there are motels...?"

"Three. One's outside the south end, about two miles out. The other two are on Linden Avenue, about a block apart," Dan answered.

"You can take me to the nearby one, if that's alright with you. I'll let you pick which one," the man tentatively said.

"Be happy to." Dan made a U-turn, headed back down the street, and turned right on Linden. After driving a couple of blocks, he pointed to a bench. "The bus stops there. I work in the drugstore across the street."

"Have you lived in town long?"

"Paul and I grew up here," Dan answered, "but our parents came from Chicago." In a few minutes, he stopped at a cluster of small cottages with bright blue roofs. "Here we are, the imaginatively named 'Farmingford Auto Court Motel.' The office is in the first cabin. If this doesn't work, the 'Mountain View' is in the next block."

"Thank you. This will be fine, I'm sure. I want to repay you for your kindness," the man pulled out his wallet. "It was so generous of you to give me a ride."

"You don't have to pay me anything," Dan waved off the offer with one hand. "Enjoy your stay in the teeming metropolis of Farmingford!"

"Well, thank you again for your assistance," the hitchhiker said.

"You're welcome, and good luck," Dan said.

The man got out of the jeep, his small suitcase in hand, and headed for the office. Dan drove the short distance to his house, parked in the driveway, and grabbed the creel. He carried the catch to a laundry sink that was attached to an outside garage wall–named "Mom's Fish Washing Station," after the brothers and their father gutted and cleaned one too many fish in the kitchen.

Paul carried the prepared trout inside, putting one in the refrigerator for Paul and the rest in the freezer. He glanced at the clock and growled. He had to hurry or he would be late for work and have to listen to grumpy Mr. Allen's standard "young people nowadays" speech.

Quickly washing his hands, he passed through the living room, stopping at the fireplace as he frequently did. A framed photograph of a smiling young man in an Army uniform rested on the mantle. Next to it hung a small, rectangular banner with a blue border and gold star.

"Miss you, Dad," Dan whispered.

Memories and emotions flooded over him. It didn't happen every time he viewed the picture, but at unpredictable moments. He remembered the dreadful time the telegram came: "Regret to inform you..." Days followed of crying, silence, disbelief, the family propping each other up, or simply not wanting to do anything at all, completely numb. Paul grew so angry that he and Dan got into their first—and only—physical fight. Soon after that, Paul started taking boxing lessons.

The striking of the mantle clock snapped Dan out of his memories. He glanced at the time and swore. He ran down the hall to his room and quickly changed into his uniform: black pants, white long sleeve shirt, black clip-on bow tie, and a red apron. He raced back out the kitchen door, locked it, then made for the jeep. He skidded to a stop.

He'd forgotten to unload it completely. With an angry cry, he opened the garage door, grabbed the fishing poles and tackle box, and stuck them inside. Then he spotted his sketchbook on the passenger side floor. Dan groaned with annoyance and snatched up the book. Something rectangular, a piece of beige pasteboard, lay under it. Dan picked up the object up and examined it.

It was the stub of a Greyhound bus ticket. Dated today.

Chapter Two

The late morning sun flooded the kitchen's breakfast nook as Paul examined the bus ticket stub. "Chicago to Greenborough. Huh." He handed it back to Dan.

"Our hitchhiker wanted to give us a tip for driving him into town. He probably dropped this when he pulled out his wallet." Dan dropped the pasteboard on the table.

"Didn't he say he was going to Omaha?" Paul stirred his coffee. "Greyhound certainly must have direct routes there from Chicago. Why go to Greenborough?"

"It could be the fare is cheaper with a transfer or something," Dan shrugged.

"Which you don't believe." Paul tapped the spoon twice against the mug's rim before laying it on the table.

"Which I don't believe," Dan nodded.

"So he got off the bus that passed us." Paul popped the last bit of toast into his mouth.

"He must have." Dan slipped the stub into his back pocket. "The southbound one wouldn't arrive there until, what, 6:00 or 6:30 at night?"

"Well, anyone can miss a bus. It's no crime." Paul drained his coffee mug. "So why tell us that story about hitchhiking?"

"Could it be he was embarrassed?" Dan shook his head. "I don't know. He may have wanted to miss it, although I can't think of a reason why."

"Perhaps he was just tired of bus travel...or wasn't feeling well. You know, carsick," Paul said.

"Our jeep rides like a bucking bronco," Dan pointed out. "If the bus made him ill, he should have turned a lovely shade of pea green by the time we reached town." He sighed. "Well, I guess our rider will remain a mystery forevermore. But boy, is it nagging at me."

Paul slid off the built-in bench and started gathering the breakfast things. "My turn to do the dishes?"

Dan smiled and waved a hand toward the sink. "That it is, my dear brother. The sink is your domain."

The phone rang. Paul putting the dishes back down then went toward the living room. "But first!"

Dan got off the bench. He heard Paul answering the phone.

"Yes, we'll accept reversed charges," Paul said. He called to Dan. "It's Mom!"

Dan hurried over to Paul. His brother held the receiver out so both could hear.

"Hi, boys!" Mom's familiar voice crackled out of the phone.

"Hi, Mom!" the twins chorused back.

"How was the train trip to Los Angeles?" Paul asked.

"It was a long!" Mom replied. "At least I was able to sleep some."

"Have you seen any movie stars out there yet?" Dan put in.

Mom chuckled. "Why, yes, of course! They're all over the place! You can't take a step without falling over one. Cary Grant carried my suitcase from the train, and Errol Flynn drove me to the hotel."

The brothers laughed. Dan asked, "How's the meeting going? Think of it—all those water department managers in one spot!"

"We just started," Mom said. "So far, just a lot of speeches."

"Are you the only woman there? There can't be that many women managers." Paul added with pride, "You were the first around these parts,"

"There's a few women, not many," Mom said. "Are you two doing all right on your own? You haven't burned down the house yet, have you?"

"Only a minor blaze in the kitchen," Dan said.

"We'll have the damage repaired, replastered and painted before you get back," Paul added.

Mom laughed. "It better be as good as new! No, better! I've got to go. You two keep out of trouble."

"We promise!" Paul said.

"I miss you two."

"We miss you too, Mom!" the boys said. "Love you!"

"Love you both! Bye!" Mom said.

"Bye!" Dan and Paul replied. Just as they hung up, the front doorbell rang.

"You're not expecting a visitor, are you?" Dan asked. Paul shook his head. "Busy day. I'll get it while you tackle the dishes. Perhaps door-to-door salesmen must be getting an early start this year." Dan started toward the living room, imitating the chipper tone of a husker. "Good morning, sir. Would you be interested in a Suck-It-Up Super Duper Vacuum Cleaner?"

Dan had the words "we don't want any" ready on his lips when he answered the door. A tall, rugged looking man with black hair streaked with gray stood at the door. "Well, no vacuum cleaner in hand. That's a good sign. Are you hawking insurance instead? Because we—"

"No, I'm not selling anything." The stranger took a wallet from his pocket, opened it, and showed Dan an identification card. "Roy Archer. I'm a private investigator representing the Worldwide Insurance Company."

"Oh?" Dan looked at the detective questioningly.

"Who is it?" Paul's voice came from the kitchen.

"A private eye," Dan yelled back.

"A what?" Paul appeared at the door, drying his hands with the dish towel.

"A private eye," Dan repeated, gesturing to Archer. "At our own front door."

"I'm looking for a pair of twins who drive a jeep." Archer rested his bright dark eyes on Dan and Paul, and then his lean face lightened in a grin. "And I guess you're them."

"We're the only ones in town. What do you want with us?" Dan asked. "Oh, I'm Dan, and this is Paul."

"I sometimes wear glasses and he doesn't. So you can tell us apart," Paul offered.

"And I'm right handed, and he's left handed." Dan added.

"And we don't dress the same, either," Paul said.

"And we don't read each other's mind," Dan summed up. "So ends the answers to the typical identical twin questions we get."

Archer chuckled. "Very helpful. Are your parents around?"

"Mom's away on a business trip," Dan said.

Paul continued. "Our Dad..." His voice faltered.

"Our Dad was killed on D-Day," Dan finished soberly.

"He didn't even get off the beach." Paul's tone was bitter.

Dan glanced at his brother. Paul focused on the floor, his hands twisting the towel into a knot.

"I'm sorry to hear about your father." Archer's eyes took on a haunted, distant look. "I served in the Pacific."

"Rough," Dan replied.

"Yeah, yeah it was," Archer responded quietly.

There was melancholy silence for a moment.

Dan snapped the mood back by swinging the door wide. "Would you like to come in?"

Archer smiled. "Yes, thank you."

The trio stepped into the living room. Archer scanned the interior with a practiced eye of a professional before he spoke.

"Right now, I need some help, in the form of information," Archer said. "I think you can give it to me, provided you two picked up a rider yesterday at Wayside Gas Station, that is. I talked to a young man who works there—"

"Ken," Dan said.

"That's it, Ken," Archer nodded. "He said he thought he saw a stranger get into your jeep."

"We gave a lift to somebody there alright," Paul took a step toward Archer. "Tall, thin, sickly looking fellow. Pale."

"That sounds like who I'm looking for." The detective reached into his coat pocket. "We can clinch the thing right now. Did you give a ride to this man?" He handed Paul a square of glossy paper bearing two pictures—side and front-view regulation police mugshots.

Paul examined the photo, nodded and handed it to Dan. "That's him, but younger."

"Absolutely." Dan passed the images back to Archer. "Who is he? What's he done?"

"Nothing, as of now," Archer returned the picture to his pocket. "So where did you—"

"What's all this about?" Dan fired off. "Who is that guy? Why are you interested in him?"

"He will not give up with the questions until he gets answers, Mr. Archer," Paul crossed his arms. "I know him too well."

"An investigator in training?" The detective cocked an eyebrow at Dan.

"I've got my junior G-Man badge in my room," Dan said with a smile. "Sent in two cereal box tops for it."

Archer grinned. "I guess information is going to have to flow both ways, then."

"If we're involved in something that wraps up a private detective with the package, you bet," Dan remarked. "I think it's a fair trade."

"You could be right. I don't believe there's any harm in telling you more," Archer said. "Have either of you heard of Lorenzo

Rizzo?" Archer looked between the brothers. They shook their heads. "Rizzo was a mob boss in Chicago during Prohibition. He started as a bootlegger, then expanded into other lines of business, such as gambling and the protection racket. Finally, he went into armed robbery."

"And that's this guy, Rizzo?" Dan pointed to Richard's pocket, which held the photo. "Seems awfully young."

"No, it's not him," Archer said. "The stock market wasn't the only thing that crashed in 1929. So did Rizzo. He and several members of his gang were gunned down in June—another version of the Saint Valentine's Day Massacre which took place earlier that year."

"Then who was our passenger, if not Rizzo?" Dan planted his fists on his hips.

"Your hitchhiker was Eddie Ridgway. He was Rizzo's bookkeeper," Archer answered.

"Bookkeeper!" Paul laughed. "I never thought of gangsters needing an accountant."

"They do. Al Capone always claimed he was a legitimate businessman. Ridgway not only had knowledge of the profit and loss from Rizzo's activities, but where the cash was stashed," Archer continued, "setting up the foreign bank accounts and such. He is very intelligent and crafty. After Rizzo's gang was cut down in a hail of submachine gun fire, Ridgway called himself Ambrose Dexter and set up shop as a financial consultant. For six years, he was quite successful at growing investments for his clients...while he skimmed money off the top for his use at the same time. When everything came to light, the final amount he embezzled was about three hundred thousand dollars."

Dan and Paul gave out with a low whistle.

"Ridgway was convicted of multiple counts of fraud and tax evasion and sent to the penitentiary. He was released last year, and had been leading a quiet life." Archer put his hands in his pockets.

"So why are you trailing him?" Dan persisted. "You said he had done nothing. He's paid his debt to society and all that."

"The problem is nobody can find any of the funds he took. Not a single dime. No bank accounts, nothing. Of course, Ridgway didn't offer any help in the matter," Archer said. "He hasn't been acting like a wealthy man, either, after his release."

"Which means he could have concealed the money somewhere as cold, hard cash, hoarding it for future use," Dan reasoned, "after everybody forgot the entire business, or statutes had run out or something."

The investigator grinned his approval. "Now you're earning your badge, junior G-Man. Ridgway had been living a quiet life—until recently. Our office received a tip that he quit his job and was moving out of his apartment. We put a tail on him and discovered he purchased a ticket to Greenborough."

"Strong clues that he was making his move to grab his cash," Dan said.

Archer nodded. "Worldwide paid out over one hundred thousand dollars in a claim to one of Ridgway's victims, and we'd like that money back. And we'll pay ten thousand dollars for information leading to its recovery. Some of the other insurance companies involved may also offer rewards."

The brothers exchanged glances, and Dan stepped forward. He gave the bus ticket to Archer. "I found it in our jeep last night. Ridgway must have accidentally dropped it."

The investigator took the stub. "Greenborough," he read.

"He approached us after the Greyhound pulled out," Paul said.

"I'm not sure how he gave me the slip back at the gas station." Archer sighed. "I'd been following the bus in my car, and when it pulled in there, I continued a few hundred feet ahead and parked in a narrow farm lane. I saw Ridgway get back on—"

"Or you thought you did," Dan noted.

"Or I thought I did," Archer agreed grimly. "So I drove on, with the bus behind me all the time. He didn't get off here in Farmingford, and there are no additional stops before Belmont. He wasn't on the bus when it reached the depot there, so I knew then he'd disappeared somehow back at that rest stop. I suppose he knew he was being tailed. He's plenty smart enough to figure that out, so he pulled this trick to shake me off. Okay, he came up to you after the bus left..."

"He didn't ask for a ride, but he seemed so helpless that we, well, we felt sorry for him and offered one," Paul explained.

"That's an act. Ridgway is an excellent confidence man," Archer said. "He fooled his financial clients for years. Then what?"

"He told us he was hitchhiking to his brother's place in...Omaha?" Dan looked at Paul for confirmation. Paul nodded.

"He doesn't have a brother, in Nebraska or anywhere else," Archer commented. "As far as I know, he has no known associates in Greenborough, either."

"Well, we drove him into town," Dan went on. "After I dropped Paul off at his job, I took Ridgway to the auto court, then came home, cleaned out the jeep and headed for work."

"Can you remember if he said anything?" Archer asked. "Even if you didn't think it was important at the time."

The brothers looked at each other for a second before Paul answered, "The only other thing I recall is that Ridgway paged through Dan's sketchbook."

"He liked my artwork," Dan told Archer. "Obviously a man of great taste."

Paul gave a half-shrug. "Debatable." He winced as Dan delivered a swift sideways kick to his ankle.

"You took him to the auto court?" Archer clarified. "Where is it?"

"Just down on Linden Avenue." Paul pointed in the direction. "I'm heading to the Belmont YMCA for some sparring practice. It'll take me past the auto court. You can follow me."

"Yeah, I'll go along to see if you have any more questions," Dan said.

"Sounds like a plan." Archer headed for the front door.

Dan and Paul piled into their jeep, Paul slipping behind the wheel while Archer climbed into a late-model blue sedan.

"See what he's driving?" Paul gave a slight jerk of his head toward Archer's shiny car. "Keep up with those Dick Tracy comics and perhaps one day, my dear brother, you too can grow up to be a detective. Then you can buy something like that."

"Better reading Dick Tracy than about that punch-drunk Joe Palooka," Dan returned.

Paul grinned as he shifted into first gear. "Ha!"

They were quiet during the short drive to the auto court. Stopping out front, Archer pulled up behind them.

"Office is in the first cabin," Dan said to the investigator as he walked by the jeep. Archer nodded and continued.

"Ten thousand dollars..." Paul said, shaking his head.

"Sitting right here in this seat," Dan completed. He thought of the bills, some marked with red "Past Due" stamps, resting in the living room desk drawer. "Mom certainly could use that money."

"You said it," Paul replied. "That's like a couple of year's salary."

"Well, we can't cry over spilled milk." Dan hopped out of the jeep.

"Let me know what happens with Archer," Paul said.

"Will do, sir." Dan snapped off a salute. "Watch out for those punches, sucker."

"You mean sucker punches," Paul corrected.

Dan grinned. "Maybe I do."

Paul clawed the air at his brother. "You're lucky you're out of reach. If I ever get my hands on you..."

Dan thumbed his nose then Paul drove off. Dan aimlessly wandered in front of the auto court until Archer emerged from the office and came over to him.

"He was there, all right," Archer said. "Even registered under his own name. Very bold. Checked out early this morning after asking about the bus." The detective scanned the small town's main street. "Could he get out of town without a car?"

"Nope. There's only one way," Dan said. "The AM buses to and from Belmont."

"Cabs?"

Dan shook his head. "No local taxis. He could have called one from Belmont, but that would be expensive."

Archer let out an irritated breath. "He didn't make any phone calls from his room."

"Maybe he hitchhiked again," Dan suggested.

"I hope not. That's pretty much untraceable." Archer took off his hat and vigorously rubbed his hair. "Unless he left the auto court and checked into that one I see down the next block...what is it? The Mountain View? To throw me off track again. If only I could be sure he got on the bus."

Dan snapped his fingers. "I think I may know a way. You see about the Mountain View, then meet me at the Allen Drug Store. It's two blocks down." Dan pointed. "The bus stop's right across the street. Ted's working this morning and I'll ask if he noticed anybody boarding."

"Why can't I go with you?"

"Ted's had a few run-ins with the local sheriff. Nothing big, just stupid stuff," Dan said, "but he's leery of questions, especially from authority figures. Like private eyes."

Archer smiled. "I have to take my hat off to you again. You're certainly earning your badge today. I'll inquire about Ridgway at the Mountain View, then meet you outside the drugstore."

Dan acknowledged Archer with a nod and walked rapidly to

Allen's Drugs. The bell over the door jingled loud and clear as he stepped in. He wound his way through the sweet aroma of the perfume shelves, past the beauty products, and neared the lunch counter running along the side wall. He gave the paperback book display a spin as he sat on a stool.

"Howdy Case." Ted, another boy about Paul's age, was wiping down the marble top with a rag. He moved down to Dan, still cleaning. He leaned in and whispered, "Careful. Old man Allen's on the warpath. Health department inspection is coming up. If he spots you here, he'll put you to work scrubbing the floors with a toothbrush on your hands and knees."

Dan laughed and glanced over his shoulder at the owner's office. The door was closed. "Safe so far. But I'm sure tonight I'll have to polish those syrup dispensers so shiny I can use them to comb my hair."

Ted chuckled. "So what brings you in early? You don't start for another six hours."

"I just wanted to know if you saw a guy in here this morning." Dan grabbed an order pad and pencil. He started to sketch.

"Why do you want to know that?" Suspicion tinged Ted's voice.

"Paul and I gave him a ride into town yesterday, and he was interested in my art. He said he might buy a landscape of mine and was going to meet me here." Dan finished the drawing, tore it off the sheet and showed the result to Ted. "This is him."

Ted examined the picture. He nodded as he handed it back to Dan. "Yeah, I remember him. He was in here. Skinny guy. Looked like a strong breeze would knock him over. Man, did he talk my ear off! Here I am in the middle of the breakfast rush, and this goober keeps going on and on about being sick and in the hospital and traveling to live with his brother in Omaha, blah blah blah. Anyway, your almost-customer climbed on the morning bus. Sorry Rembrandt, you lost a sale."

"Oh, too bad." Dan hoped he sounded suitably disappointed. "Are you sure he got on?"

"I saw what I saw when I saw it." Ted folded his arms and leaned against the counter. "He took a seat in the back. Watched him through the windows. I felt sorry for whoever got stuck next to him, the way he talked." He suddenly straightened up. "Allen's door is opening. Clear out while you still have the chance."

"Thanks, Ted." Dan darted outside. As the door shut behind him, he heard a whistle. Turning toward the sound, he noticed the blue sedan parked at the end of the block. He jogged to the car. When he reached it, the passenger door popped open and Dan climbed in.

"Well?" Archer asked.

Dan shook his head. "Ridgway left on the morning bus."

"Your friend said that?"

"Yes." Dan showed the sketch he made to Archer. "Identified him and everything. Ted said Ridgway even fed him the line about his brother and going to Omaha."

"He said the same thing to the desk clerk as well." Archer stared out the windshield. "Your friend was positive Ridgway got onboard?"

"Completely. He even told me which seat he took."

"Damn. That means I have to travel to Belmont and see if I can pick up his trail again." Archer dug into his coat pocket, pulled out a business card and gave it to Dan. "If you or Paul think of anything, call my office. I check in with them daily."

Dan read the information and nodded. "Sure thing."

"Thanks, Dan, for all your assistance. And give my appreciation to Paul, too." The investigator stuck out his hand.

Dan took it, and they shook. "I'm sorry we couldn't be of more help. Good luck with the hunt."

He got out of the car. Its powerful engine roared to life, and the sedan glided down the street. Dan stood still for a moment before sighing and starting back home. He couldn't spend the several hours before he began the work day regretting how he might have earned that pretty reward if he hadn't let Ridgway slip away.

Chapter Three

D an stepped outside the Allen Drug Store that night. The door shut and locked behind him, then the shade zipped down the window. He pulled off his clip-on bow tie and let out a long, tired breath.

The sky hung low and snug, a dark blue blanket over the small town. The warm orange glow of streetlights spread across the sidewalk and the other storefronts on the street closed for the night. It was quiet, with only the sounds of the distant whistle of a train, and some children laughing somewhere in the nearby park on the next block. He heard the approach of a familiar motor, and stepped to the curb as Paul braked the jeep to a stop, the brakes squealing slightly.

"Thanks for picking me up." Dan climbed into the passenger seat. "Boy, I'm glad Ted warned me about Mr. Allen. The old man was a holy terror tonight about that health inspection. I had to clean everything twice. How did sparring go?" Paul didn't seem to be listening to him, but had his eyes glued to the rear-view mirror. Dan automatically glanced behind him. "What's up?"

"So we gave this Ridgway guy that ride into town yesterday..."

Paul began.

"Yeah."

"After we picked him up, a black delivery van passed us, remember?" Paul peered over his shoulder.

"Yeah. It sat on our bumper for a while first," said Dan. "Why?"

Paul faced his brother. "Don't you dare laugh, but I think it followed me back from Beaumont."

"All the way home?"

"No," Dan said. "When I turned on our street, it kept going straight."

"And you're sure it was the same van," Dan said.

"I'm almost positive it was."

"Well, there must be more than one black delivery van in this area."

"Well, yes, of course there is, but..."

"I mean, why would it follow you?" Dan asked.

Paul shrugged.

Dan thought for a second. "Here's what I think happened. It isn't every day we give a ride to an embezzler and receive a visit from a private detective, true?"

Paul nodded.

"Because of that, you're probably just noticing things now you wouldn't have paid any attention to before," Dan said. "You know, you buy a certain color of shirt and suddenly it seems everybody is wearing the same one. You're just more aware of it, that's all."

Paul considered the idea for a moment. "I guess that's most likely it. Makes sense. Oh, speaking of investigators, what did Archer uncover? Anything?"

Dan shook his head and told his brother what had happened with the private investigator and Ted.

Paul spread his hands. "Well, that ends our brush with the infamous."

"Think of it this way. We'll have a wonderful story to bore our kids with." Dan imitated an old man's voice, "Why, when I was a young 'un, I once gave a ride to this guy who stole fifty million dollars, by cracky!" The brothers laughed. "Do you think we can grab a burger at the drive-in? I didn't eat tonight at work. I didn't want to dirty a thing and bring down the wrath of Mr. Allen upon my head."

"We have just enough time," Paul said. "I haven't eaten either."

"No?"

"Betty phoned this afternoon," Paul flashed a slightly embarrassed smile. "We talked for a while...you know, about stuff."

"It must have been quite a while, my dear brother," Dan raised an eyebrow.

"Only a couple of hours or so," Paul said. "Then she told me she could use the family's new convertible tomorrow and asked if I wanted to go swimming at the lake with her."

"...if I wanted to go swimming at the lake with her," Dan mimicked with a lovesick sigh. He clasped his hands in front of him and batted his eyelashes as he leaned toward his twin.

"Ah, go on with you!" Paul slapped Dan's shoulder with the back of his hand. "You're just jealous!"

Dan grinned. "You bet your life I am, lover boy." He pointed forward with both index fingers. "But first, food! I can't listen to your romances on an empty stomach!"

***

Dan walked into Paul's room the next morning. "Here's the spare towel."

"Thanks." Paul examined himself in the bureau mirror, carefully combing his brown hair, making sure each strand was in its proper place. "Put it in my bag, will you please?"

Paul's gym bag sat on the bed, emptied of its usual boxing contents. Dan stuffed the towel inside, along with a swim suit, sneakers, and a transistor radio. He straightened up and grinned at his brother. He sneaked up behind Paul and mussed up his hair.

"Hey!" Paul howled.

"That's what you're going to look like after the ride in Betty's convertible, anyway!" Dan laughed.

Paul's shove sprawled Dan onto the bed. Paul leaned over, playfully pummeling Dan as his brother laughed and screamed in mock terror. "Take that! And that and that and that!"

A horn sounded from outside.

"That's her!" Paul dragged the comb through his hair. "Thou shall have a full taste of my revenge on some future date!" He grabbed his gym bag and scrambled out the door.

"Have a good time!" Dan called out.

"Thanks!" came the rushed reply.

Dan ran to the window, watched his brother climb into Betty's white convertible and drive off. With a smile, he went to the work-shop the two shared, built along one side of their home's detached garage. A punching bag, its canvas a bruised, dusty dark brown, dominated one half of the narrow room. The floor beneath it was marked with countless scrapes where Paul had scuffed it, trying to perfect his footwork. Above a few barbells resting on the linoleum, jump ropes, boxing gloves and magazine photos of professional boxers hung on the wall.

The other part of the space contained Dan's easel, placed by the only window, his stool standing in front. It was an old oak one, worn where he sat and rested his feet, but polished well enough to reflect the light coming through the glass. A table by the door had seen better days; years in the company of paint had covered it with colorful stains and its legs bowed with time and use. Dan's sketchbooks were stacked in one corner of the tabletop, newest additions on top, older ones filling in underneath.

He sat to resume work on a particularly tricky section of the landscape he was painting. After a glance at the reference photo he took of the scene, he chewed the end of the brush he held as he shifted his gaze back to the canvas.

The phone interrupted his thought. He had been so involved in his work he didn't know how long it had been ringing. Putting down his brush, he ran inside the house and snatched up the receiver. "Hello?"

"Dan, he's out here. I saw him." Paul's voice was quiet, as though trying not to be overheard.

"Paul? Is that you? Who is where? Is Betty's jealous ex-boyfriend out there with a shotgun or something?" Dan asked.

"No, not that," Paul snapped. "Ridgway. I spotted Ridgway."

"What!" Dan said. "Is this like the van? Are you—"

"No, I'm not completely sure, but this guy certainly looked a lot like him."

Dan was about to make a joke, but stopped. He knew his brother well enough that he was being sincere. "Where? Is he still there? What happened?"

"The lake's packed, but I think I saw him back by the vacation cottages. He—" Paul was quiet for a second as if distracted, then went on. "He seemed to be heading toward Wolf Lodge."

"Wolf Lodge? What would he want—" Dan started.

"We have to leave in about thirty minutes. Betty starts work at two," Paul spoke quickly. "Get out here and see if you can find him. If it is Ridgway, we can call Archer and—"

"Have a shot at claiming that reward money," Dan finished. "I'll head out now. I should make it before you have to go, but if not, stall Betty until I arrive. Meanwhile, keep your eyes peeled. See if he comes back down."

"Do I tell you about Ridgway in front of Betty?"

"No. The fewer people know about this, the better." Dan thought for a second. "Tell you what. Remember how you used to annoy me when we were kids? You would reflect light off your glasses in my face?"

"Yes."

"I'll wear my red trunks," Dan said, "and swim out to the float. When you see me, reflect the sun on your glasses. One flash means he's come down, two flashes mean he hasn't. If he has, I'll stay to scout around to see if I can hunt him up. If not, I'll go up to the lodge to see if I can uncover something."

"Got it. Hurry." Paul hung up.

Dan race up to his room and quickly changed into his swimming suit, tee-shirt and sneakers. Bounding downstairs, he executed a perfect flying leap into the jeep and headed for the Glenstall Park. Twenty-five minutes later, he pulled into the parking lot.

Nestled away outside town, the state park held an abundance of twisting mountain paths and rolling hills, and was summer-busy today. The campground was bustling with activity and most of the day-use areas were almost full.

Dan parked and hopped out of the jeep, stopping a second to take in a deep, grateful breath of the woodsy aroma of the trees and the sweet, grassy meadows. He took off his shoes and his shirt, tossing them into the back seat. He headed toward the beach, the sun-warmed ground pleasant under foot.

Arrowhead Lake was roughly triangular, as the name implied. Tall, rocky cliffs rimmed two sides of the lake, while a sandy shore filled the base of the triangle. The water, so clear he could see the fish in the depths, cast a mirror-like reflection of the bluffs and woods. A few kayaks and canoes floated out in the lake, their wakes wrinkling the surface. Some children swam from a small, floating dock that was anchored a little offshore.

Dan splashed into the lake, swimming to the float. He climbed aboard, dripping water, and scanned the crowded beach. A collection of cottages, standing in clusters of two and three, lay in an arc just behind the sand, looking like doll houses under the tall trees. A larger building stood nearer the shore, bright beneath a skirt of pine needles. It held the resort office, store and snack bar, its sign advertising hot dogs, ice cream, and sodas. A whiff of grilled meat reached all the way out to Dan. To one side, an immaculate white structure hosted the restrooms, in which were also public shower and changing rooms.

It took a few minutes before Dan picked out his brother and Betty in the mass of beach goers. They sat on the sand in their swim suits, laughing. Betty got up and headed to the changing rooms. Paul stood and looked toward the float. He waved at Dan, and Dan returned a wave. Paul took off his glasses; two flashes of reflected sun. Scooping up the towels, Paul walked toward the white building.

Dan dove back into the water and returned to shore. Back at the jeep, he quickly toweled himself off, then slipped on his sneakers and tee-shirt. He hurried in the direction of the trail leading to Wolf Lodge.

Threading its way among rocks and trees, the first part of the well-maintained trail was meant for non-hiking tourists and climbed uphill slightly. He met a family of four coming in the opposite direction, which included one teenage girl. She caught Dan's eye, smiled at him approvingly and playfully, an impish grin that blossomed into a full-blown smile when he stepped off the trail to let them by. He shyly returned the grin, hoping the blood rushing to his cheeks didn't show.

Before the trail curved back to the parking lot, it touched a dirt road. Gated down at the highway, this once-graveled drive snaked its way up to the lodge. A rabbit hopped from under the trees onto the road, looked around with a jerk of his brown head, and then streaked off into the undergrowth. Dan turned on the drive and continued, breathing a little hard when he finally crested the top.

Wolf Lodge could have swallowed three houses the size of Dan's with room to spare. Stone walls rose two stories high and a broad porch extended clear across the front of the building, providing a magnificent view of the surrounding mountains. A great place to lounge and look over the lake on a warm summer day, Dan thought. Twenty-five yards from the porch, the bluff dropped twenty feet straight down to the waters of Arrowhead Lake.

Smoke scars, now fading, still were visible on the walls above the now boarded-up windows and doors. A few blackened, skeletal rafters could be seen towering above the second floor, starkly silhouetted against the blue sky, a dark harbinger of the flaming chaos that had once reigned inside.

Dan paced the length of the lodge, speculating on what Ridgway—if Paul had indeed seen him—would want at the old building. Then he wondered what he would say if he ran into Ridgway coming the other way—"I didn't expect to meet you here" or "Find all your cash yet?" Could he even conceal that he knew about the hitchhiker's past?

He hoped he didn't have to find out as he turned the corner and walked down the side of the building, consisting of more scorched walls and blocked windows. He reached the back of the lodge. Off to the rear, untouched by the fire, stood an outbuilding, also built of stone. He didn't have to get close to notice the padlock on the door.

A rustling in the trees caused him to turn around. Two hikers emerged from the woods and passed him, heading to the drive. As Dan and the duo exchanged greetings, he recalled the multiple paths and old logging roads that crisscrossed the park. Ridgway could have been coming *toward* the lodge, but not *to* it, Dan realized. He may have just walked by and proceeded along any one of the other trails, like those hikers. Dan wasn't Daniel Boone; he couldn't track Ridgway through the wilderness, or even determine if he had been here at all. Nothing more could be done now. He returned to the jeep and drove home.

The sound of thwack-thwack-thwack came from the workshop as Dan parked the jeep. He walked over and opened the door. Paul stood in the far end of the room, concentrating as he rhythmically battered the hanging punching bag, his arms taut and strong, as he swung his fists in neat arcs. Dan became mesmerized watching the blurry bag rocking back and forth, so much that he started when Paul held on to it and it stopped.

"Well?" Paul asked. "Was he there?"

Dan shrugged. "I didn't see Ridgway at the lodge. Just ran into a couple of hikers."

"I could have sworn it was him," Paul muttered.

"Of course, you could have been so intoxicated by Betty's beauty that you hallucinated the whole thing." Dan grinned. "Not that I would blame you, but I think not."

Paul inclined his head in thanks. "Do you believe I saw him?"

"I believe you thought you did, but it could have been a case of mistaken identity." Dan sighed. "At least I hope you had a good time. It looked like you two were having fun."

"We did," Paul smiled.

"Well, I'm off to toil behind a hot soda fountain," Dan said. "See you later."

It was a busy night at the drug store. Several groups of kids from Dan's school came to play the jukebox and dance. He hustled behind the counter and to the few tables, serving sodas and hot fudge sundaes. He even tried to banter and flirt with a group of girls, and, as usual, failed miserably. Despite that, Dan enjoyed the evening, playing the host of the party, and was still grinning as he cleaned up after closing. Unfortunately, he thought as he converted a handful of coins into bills at the cash register, his fellow students were lousy tippers.

Dan finished readying for the morning opening. Waving to the cashier and pharmacist, he turned and left the store. The day's heat still clung to the night air. He pulled off his bow tie and dropped it in his pocket as he unbuttoned the top three buttons on his shirt. He headed toward the jeep parked on the next block. Dan had just reached it when a voice caused him to jump.

"Hey, kid..."

A man materialized out of the shadows of a nearby doorway. He stepped into the puddle of light thrown from the street lamp.

"Sorry, I didn't see you in the dark," Dan said, although he immediately wondered how he could have missed him.

The man was large, almost as big as a football player. His hair was red and mowed short. His face lay half in shadow, but it was clear the man's nose had been broken more than once. A thin scar ran down his right cheek. He wore a gray suit and hat, its brim tugged over his eyes.

"That's all okay." The stranger's voice was raspy, with a rusty hinge quality. He seemed to study Dan's face before continuing. "Nice night, ain't it?"

"Yes it is," Dan said.

The stranger pulled out a cigarette from his inside coat pocket and stuck it between his lips. "Gotta light?"

"Sorry, no I don't," Dan said. "I don't smoke."

The man took the cigarette out of his mouth and dismissed Dan with a wave. "That's okay, pal." He brushed past Dan and walked around the corner with a pronounced limp.

Dan waited for a moment, then peeked around the edge of the building. The man was walking down the sidewalk, stopped, and yanked a lighter from inside his coat. Flicking it, a tiny flame burst from the top. He lit his smoke, the glow outlining his head in orange. The man took a deep drag, breathing out a plume of blue smoke. He continued to the end of the block and turned the corner.

Chapter Four

Sunlight streamed through the workshop window early the next morning, highlighting the dust particles in the air. Dan leaned into his canvas, his deft brush strokes blending shades of blue and purple together in a mesmerizing effect. Paul grunted as he hefted dumbbells up and down in repetition.

"I can't help but keep wondering." Dan leaned back on his stool, chewing the wooden end of his brush.

"Wondering what?" Paul blew out his breath as he raised the weights.

"If you spotted Ridgway yesterday or not," Dan said.

"Well, that's what it seemed like at the time." Paul put the dumbbells down on the floor with a dull thud. "Here, help me with my sit-ups."

Paul laid down on the floor. Dan got on his knees and held his brother's feet. "Was it far from where you and Betty were sitting when you sighted him?"

"Yeah," Paul admitted as he started his exercise.

Dan thought for a second. "Did Ridgway make any sign that he recognized you?"

"No," Paul puffed out. "You saw...how crowded it was. I...doubt he picked me out...of everybody...on the beach."

"Come on, buddy, all the way up. Elbows touch the knees," Dan coached.

"Taskmaster," Paul grunted out. "I'm sorry...I sent you...on a wild goose...chase."

"It may not have been. I mean, it could have been your imagination acted up, like with the van. Not wanting Ridgway to slip through our fingers twice, you thought you saw him," Dan said. "Stop."

Paul flopped back on the floor with a groan. "Should we call Archer, anyway?"

Dan frowned as he shook his head. "We need more to work with if we're going to prove that Ridgway is here. Right now all we have is a potential sighting, which gives us two options. Either the person at the lake actually was Ridgway, or it was somebody who just looks like him. It's not that unheard of for two people to bear a strong resemblance to one another. Or so I've been told."

Paul grinned, sat up, and wrapped his arms around his knees. "Maybe Ridgway's got a twin too."

"Nah, that's something out of bad mystery stories." Dan waved off the idea.

"You've read enough of them."

Dan laughed, then continued, "But I'll bet you're thinking what I'm thinking."

"You mean that if Ridgway is still in Farmingford and we're the only ones who know it, then that reward money is as good as ours right now?" Paul hinted.

Dan nodded. "Uh-huh."

"The idea never entered my mind." Paul put on an angelic expression.

"The idea never entered your mind, my great maiden aunt Fanny!" Dan gave Paul's shoulder a push.

"Okay, perhaps the barest inkling of the vestige of the idea flashed through my brain," Paul allowed with a smile.

"But we need to figure out if Ridgway is still in town or not, whether your sighting was accurate," Dan said. "That's where we need to start."

Paul tapped his forehead with an index finger. "My gray matter may have cooked up a way."

Dan cocked an eyebrow. "I didn't know doing all those exercises increased your smarts as well. If that's true, you should be an Einstein by now."

Paul got up. "Put away your paint box, my dear brother, and I'll show you how my brain size is equal to my bulging biceps."

"I'm going to barf," Dan said.

Paul snapped his fingers and pointed to the ground as he headed for the door. "Heel."

Dan shot his brother a quizzical glance, then followed Paul to the living room. Paul picked up the phone book and flipped through some pages. He looked up a listing and handed the book to Dan.

"Get me the number for the Mountain View Motel," Paul directed, as he sat in the desk chair and dialed the phone. "Hello? Farmingford Auto Court? Please connect me to Eddie Ridgway's room." He listened for a minute. "Oh, he's not registered? Thank you. Must have been my mistake." He hung up. "One down, three to go. Where's the Mountain View?"

Dan showed his brother the line on the page. Paul nodded. "Now find the one between here and Belmont...the Midway Motel, I think it's called." He dialed the number. "Mountain View Motel? Please connect me to Eddie Ridgway's room." He waited, adjusting his glasses. "He's not registered? Sorry, must have been my mistake." He put down the receiver. "Midway." Paul checked the entry Dan had his finger on, then placed the call. "Arrowhead Lake Resort," he ordered. The last two calls had the same result as the first two.

"So there is nobody registered as Eddie Ridgway at any of those places?" Dan asked.

Paul shook his head as he pushed the phone away. "Which means we can ditch any hypothesis that Ridgway is trying to fool Archer by doubling back here again and using his real name like he did before."

"Okay, that leaves two other possibilities." Dan paced the floor. "One, he's gone, left on the bus and never came back, and there's a look-alike out at the resort. Or two, he's registered under an assumed name." He threw his hands up in despair. "How do we find that out? We somehow split ourselves into four people to stake out all the motels and try to spot him?"

"I saw him at the lake. Let's start there." Paul stood, then groaned. "I can't go out now. I have to do the Walters' and Fentons' lawns today."

"Well, I have tonight off. I could go…" Dan shook his head. "No, that won't work. We can't just perch out there like a couple of vultures. The more we hang around out there, the more likely Ridgway could spot us if he's staying there. And he knows our jeep, too, remember. It's the only one like it around here."

"True."

"Here's one more observation: he could have already picked up the cash yesterday, checked out, and scrammed." Dan shrugged in resignation. "If we could peek at the resort's register, that could give us some idea."

Paul snapped his fingers. "There may be a way we can!" He sat down again, pulled the phone to him, and lifted the receiver. "I just need to call Betty…" He looked at Dan and jerked his head toward the door in a silent order.

Dan bowed low, arms spread wide as he backed out of the room. "But of course, sire. I understand the not-so-subtle command to withdraw. Your humble servant will allow Don Juan Caseanova to whisper sweet nothings into his sweetheart's ears alone."

He stepped outside and took in the fresh morning air. He imagined his mother's expression when the twins presented her with a check for ten thousand dollars. She had done her best to protect the brothers from the truth of their financial struggles since their father's death, but he and Paul knew every penny counted. The thought of surprising her with a windfall was too good to be true.

Paul came out onto the porch. "It's all set. Betty's friend Donna works summers at the resort in the store. She may be able to get access to the guest register, since it sits behind the reception desk."

"That's great!" Dan went up to his brother. "I'll get that drawing of Ridgway I did for Ted, and then we will—"

"Not we, you." Paul pointed at Dan. "I'll have to hustle to get those lawns done today. The Walters are sticklers about the schedule, especially because Mrs. Walters is holding some kind of garden party shindig tomorrow. Besides, part of the deal is that Donna wants to talk to you. Alone."

"Alone?" Dan gulped.

"Yes. For some peculiar reason, she's told Betty that you're cute...like a cocker spaniel. Those are her words." Paul crossed his arms and titled his head as he regarded his brother. "Must be your soft brown eyes. Or maybe it's the floppy ears."

"I wish to point out you have the same set of ears," Dan declared.

"Well, for whatever crazy idea, I think she's interested in you," Paul smirked.

"In me? But...but she's...she's beautiful and...and a cheerleader," Dan sputtered. "I mean, the cheerleaders go for football or basketball players, not guys like me...you know, non-athlete nobodies. She's out of my league."

Paul put his arm around his brother and pulled him close. "And she requested you wear your red swim trunks. So she can recognize you."

"Recognize me!" Dan exclaimed. "We go to the same small high school together! She knows exactly what I look like! You, minus the glasses!"

"Well, that's what she wants. Oh, and here's the best part: I agreed we would go all on a double date afterwards," Paul whispered.

"What!" Dan said. "Paul...Paul, you know how awkward I am around girls...especially pretty ones like Donna...I never know what to say...what to do..." He pushed his brother away. "You're enjoying watching my discomfort and embarrassment, aren't you?"

Paul folded his arms and grinned. "Immeasurably." He mussed up Dan's hair and darted to the porch steps. He struck a triumphant pose. "And now, knave, knowest thou that revenge hath been delivered!" He cackled in his best villain voice and rubbed his hands together. "Ah! What a sweet dish it is!"

"I hate you," Dan fired back. "I wonder if it's too late to trade you in for a different model."

"Have confidence in yourself, Dan. Remember that Mark Twain quote Dad used to tell us? 'Do the thing you fear the most and the death of fear is certain?'"

Dan smiled and nodded. "Yes. Okay. All right, I'll talk to Donna."

"That's the spirit! I guess I'll walk over the Walters first, since it's only a few blocks away. And, my dear brother, just the red bathing suit..." Paul poked an elbow in Dan's direction, winked, and clucked his tongue a couple of times. "...you good lookin' dog you." He gave a wolf howl.

The daily newspaper lay on the porch. Dan picked it up and flung it at Paul as his twin scooted around the corner of the house.

Dan went to his room and retrieved his red trunks from the bureau. As he dressed, he glanced at his reflection in the mirror.

He stood and stared at himself.

"A cocker spaniel?" he muttered to himself, then stepped into the hallway and pulled on his tee-shirt.

***

It was even busier at the lake than yesterday, and it took a few trips through the parking lot before he managed to find a spot. If Ridgway was staying in one cottage, Dan didn't want to be seen, so he approached the store from the crowded shore.

Threading his way through a minefield of people on the beach, dodging the running children and their flashing beach balls, Dan ended up on the steps leading to the store's porch. The cool breeze blew in from the lake and whipped around him, lifting sand and dust off the ground and into his eyes. He wiped his face clean and stopped.

"Just the red bathing suit," he muttered to himself. For the first time he could remember, he felt self-conscious about wearing swim trunks. He smoothed his tee-shirt with his hands, and tugged at the swim suit as though it was a tuxedo. "All right, here goes." He took a deep breath and walked to the screen door, holding it open for a family charging out. He stepped inside, the door squeaking and slamming behind him, waiting for his eyes to become adjusted to the light.

The resort's store stocked a mix of items, from souvenir pennants to t-shirts and sweatshirts to a refrigerated case full of beer and milk. Additional shelves held the boxed food stuffs, supplies and toilet paper needed by the campers. A lilting voice came from the counter.

"Dan!"

He turned. Donna stood by the cash register, wearing a plaid button-down shirt, the kind that old men wear to their grandkid's baseball games, and jeans, with a "Howdy! I'm Donna!" name tag pinned to the collar. Her auburn hair was cut short and wisped out around her ears. Her blue eyes, smoky and soulful, sparkled.

"Hi, Donna," Dan squeezed out, sounding to him like a mouse squeaking. All at once, he didn't know what to do with his hands. They must have stuck out five miles long. He tried to put them in his pockets before remembering his swim suit only had one in the back, so he folded his arms across his chest and walked over to the counter.

"So, what's the big deal?" Donna smiled. Dan melted. "Betty made it sound like you and Paul were detectives or something!"

Dan cleared his throat and a dry chuckle emerged. "Nothing like that. It's just...ah...Paul thought he saw a friend of our Dad's out here yesterday. An...an old Army buddy of his. Yeah. They graduated from basic training together. We wanted to make sure so we can...ah...surprise him."

Donna gave Dan a knowing look. "If you say so."

"Yeah, well...oh, here." He took his sketch out of his wallet. "He looks like this."

Even though he held the paper out front, Donna walked around the counter to stand next to him. Her flowery perfume wafted over him, tingling his nostrils. She grasped his hand and gently pulled it toward her so she could see the picture.

"Did you draw this?" Donna asked.

His voice cracked. "Uh-huh." He cleared his throat and continued, hoping he sounded matter of fact. "It's just a quick sketch I sketched, um, quickly."

"That's really good. You've got quite a talent," she cooed.

"Thanks." Dan nervously giggled, then felt more relaxed. "Have you seen him?"

Donna shook her head. "Sorry, no, but I only work three days a week, and not all the guests come in here."

"Oh." Dan couldn't hide the disappointment.

"But I did do something for you that could get me fired!" Donna whispered in a conspiratorial tone. She winked and returned to the counter. She took a sheet of paper from under the cash register and slid it to Dan. "Here's a list of the guest staying here and their cabin numbers."

Dan smiled back. "Thanks, that's great of you." He scanned the names; no Ridgway was on the list. "Anybody leave in the past couple of days, or last-minute arrivals?"

"I don't know about check outs yesterday or the day before. I wasn't here, but I'm positive there weren't any walk-in registrations. Tourists book this place solid for the entire summer. If you don't have a reservation by March, forget it," Donna answered.

"Well, I guess Paul didn't really see this guy after all." Dan folded the paper and slipped in his back pocket. He and Donna stood silently, gazing at each other with slight smiles playing on their faces. "Yes, well, thank you."

"You're welcome. I'm sorry it didn't work out...about your father's friend, that is," Donna responded. Another pause. "You should stay for a swim. It's hot enough."

"Yeah, yeah it is. I mean, I have my trunks on, so I'm dressed...or undressed, for it," Dan half-laughed as he tugged at his tee-shirt collar. Even though he had completed his business, he didn't want to go. At last, he waved. "Well, thanks again. See you around."

"You're welcome again. See you. I've got to stock some shelves." Donna waved back. As Dan turned to leave, she added, "I'm looking forward to that double date with Paul and Betty."

Dan grinned. "Yeah, yeah, so am I. Well, see ya."

"Bye."

Leaving the store, Dan still had the silly grin plastered on his face. He had spoken to the prettiest girl he knew and hadn't made a fool of himself. Well, mostly. He felt more comfortable and confident, believing that she liked him even a little. The fact that Ridgway's name didn't appear on the resort's registration didn't seem to matter that much anymore. He reminded himself that's why he was there.

He peered at the list again, eyes skimming through each name to see if they missed Ridgway the first time. No, they hadn't. He let out a resigned breath and his fingers moved to crumple up the list, but he willed himself to stop. Instead, he folded the paper with care and tucked it into his pocket. Still, he believed Paul when he said he thought he saw the man.

Dan decided to explore the other areas of the resort; perhaps lightning would strike twice. Donna only said she hadn't seen him and not all the guests go to the store. He strolled away down a path, kicking up dirt with each step as he walked.

Dan took a different route toward the parking lot, walking along the pebbled walkway towards the little cabins. Now and then, a rustle came from the forest, or a chipmunk dashed across the path. Meanwhile, laughter and the sound of splashing drifted in from the beach. He trudged by the neat little cottages, all with brightly painted shutters, but nothing seemed suspicious. Dan's spirits were faltering until he spied one cabin tucked at the end of the row. While its neighbors had open windows to let in the fresh air, this one's were shut with the curtains tightly drawn. Dan wondered what—or who—could hide behind those thick brown drapes, especially on such a beautiful day.

As he stared at the cottage's door, it unexpectedly opened, and Ridgway's figure emerged. Dan whipped around as he tugged up his tee-shirt over his head, only finishing the task when his back was toward Ridgway and had moved several steps away. After he took it off, he pretended to mop his face with the bottom of the tee-shirt, keeping Ridgway in sight as the thin man rounded the corner of another nearby cottage.

Dan stumbled after him, his heart pounding, and willed himself to slow down his breathing. He couldn't believe he had almost crashed into Ridgway. He peered around the edge of the building and spotted him walking away towards the Wolf Lodge trail. His tall frame held a creel slung over one shoulder but carried no fishing pole. Dan pulled on his tee-shirt.

He got ready to follow, glanced down, and groaned. He had put his shirt on wrong, inside out and backwards. Swearing under his breath, he yanked it off, and spun it the right way, and pulled it back on. A line from a Sherlock Holmes story he once read popped into his mind.

"The game's afoot," he said to himself, and took off after Ridgway.

Chapter Five

Dan scurried up the path, using groups of tourists ahead of him as cover. He moved quickly but carefully, taking moments to scan his surroundings for any sign of detection before pushing onward. With each jogging step, he grew closer to his target, determined not to lose Ridgway from sight. He tracked his quarry up the winding drive until they reached the top.

From a crouched position behind some bushes, Dan spied on Ridgway as he turned the far edge of the lodge. Not making a sound, Dan hurried across the clearing and crept along the porch. From the other side of the building, Ridgway's slow, measured steps crunching on the dirt faded, and a faint scuffling coming from the back of the building replaced them. Dan held still and counted to twenty. Taking in a deep breath, he edged closer to the corner and peeped around. Ridgway wasn't in view.

Dan slinked down the wall, his back brushing against the boards nailed over the windows as he advanced, straining to detect any hint of being spotted. From inside, there was a slight thud, like a small object being knocked over, and he froze in place. He listened intently, but all he could hear was the running water sound of the wind in the nearby trees.

When he reached the rear of the lodge, he stopped and looked around. The plywood panel covering the back door caught his eye. He stepped forward and peered into the shadows, noticing that the board's edges didn't match up with the doorframe, as if someone had moved it. He ran his finger along the edge of the wood: someone had pried it off. There were no nails keeping it in place, but it was still leaning against the door, making it seem untouched from a distance.

Dan pressed his ear to the narrow gap between the door and the plywood which barricaded it. The faint sound of something shifting in the rooms beyond came to him. His pulse raced as he inched the wood away from the door, just enough to slip through. He gingerly maneuvered himself through the tiny opening, like a letter delivered through a mail slot.

The pungent smell of burnt wood greeted him as he stepped into the shadowy darkness of the kitchen. He took a moment to let his eyes adjust, then checked out the room. It was now bare of anything but counters, cabinets and the sink. And dirt. Lots and lots of dirt.

Four years ago, the state acquired the property the lodge sat on as an addition to Glenstall Park. The local historical society grew concerned that the building might be demolished and wanted to make a record of its interior. On his art teacher's recommendation, they hired Dan to take pictures and draw sketches of the various rooms. It was the first time he'd ever been paid for his artwork, and he devoted almost a week to the project. His memory of the floor plan returned, so the door in front of him should lead to the dining area. He crept up to the doorway and peered through—he was right!

The fire hadn't destroyed the entire structure, so this part of the building was more or less intact. The dining room shared two of the stone exterior walls, the plaster on the interior was cracked but stubbornly holding on. Soot and dust covered the exposed wooden beams. Slabs of plywood blocked the windows, and a thick layer of dirt, grime, and cobwebs coated the frames. The broken glass hadn't been removed; it lay in glittering shards on the floorboards.

Dan saw nothing that could have made the noise, so he listened again. Only the stabbing caw of a crow floated in from outside. He picked his way across the debris-strewn floor toward a partially opened double door, being careful not to make any sound in case Ridgway actually was inside and he wasn't really tracking a chipmunk.

He found himself in a wide hall that was square and roomy. Scorch marks streaked the wood paneling on the opposite wall where the flames had reached. At the far end stood a staircase running up to what had been a second story, but most of the roof had collapsed, leaving only jagged walls and piles of rubble.

Dan stood in the hallway, his eyes darting through the shadows. He inched ahead, using his feet to test each step forward. He pressed himself next to another open doorway, held his breath, and a soft rustling came from somewhere else in the building. Dan poked his head around the door frame, his heart pounding in his chest.

He was looking into the living room. It was one large space with a massive fireplace in the middle of one inside wall. Rows of windows took up the corner walls. The area was trashed—white, sooty glass, bits of burnt wood and dirt everywhere. The ceiling and roof were gone, open to the sky. Leaves, twigs and branches had fallen through the huge gape and carpeted the floor.

And, it was clear, nobody else was there.

As Dan entered the room, his heart sank. He had photographed and drawn this room when it was as beautiful as any place could be. Now it had been turned into charcoal and blackened wood. The rustic mantel was charred, and the tall bookcases flanking it reduced to jumbled boards. The tall windows that once offered a stunning view of the mountains were now sealed like a tomb. Something caught his eye.

The creel Ridgway had carried sat in front of the fireplace, its lid open, revealing a roll of paper. A pencil lay next to it.

Dan heard a faint snap from behind him. As Dan turned, something struck him in the temple. A second later, the floor rushed up to meet him, then there was blackness.

***

Sometime later, Dan groaned as his eyes cracked open. He blinked them a couple of times to get them to focus. He looked around. The shadows thrown by the sun streaming through the ruined roof had shifted only a little. It may have seemed like an eternity, but he must have only been unconscious for a few minutes. His head pounded and felt like it had split in half.

He attempted to rise, but something kept him pinned down. With one hand, he reached behind him until he grasped onto a piece of wooden debris. He yanked at it, but it wouldn't budge—so he army-crawled from beneath the weight instead, huffing and puffing with exhaustion by the time he was free. He plunked his head down on the dirty floor, closed his eyes, and rested for a moment. At last he sat up, groaning in pain as he did so. His forehead was tacky to the touch. He gasped as he looked at his fingers: blood.

Dan turned around and gazed upon the pile of burnt wood and charred plaster that had been a wall of the upper story. It must have collapsed and buried him beneath it. For a second, he forgot why he came inside the lodge.

"Oh, yeah, Ridgway, Ridgway," he muttered.

He climbed to his feet in stages and stood, swaying a bit. His gaze wandered around the room, stopping at the fireplace. The hearth was vacant. Something was there, but now he just couldn't recall what exactly. He glanced through the missing ceiling to what remained of the second floor. Empty. Walking in a more or less straight line, Dan retraced his steps to the kitchen door. He slipped past the plywood barricade and stepped outside, holding his hand up to block the sunlight, which appeared to have grown brighter.

His head pounded as he trudged down the path as he tried to reach the jeep. He pushed forward, hoping he wouldn't pass out again, determined to make it back to his house. As he rounded the last curve, he grinned in relief—the jeep sat only a few feet away.

Climbing in and collapsing against the steering wheel, he shut his eyes and allowed himself a moment of rest before starting the engine. The drive back was like driving through a red, pulsating mist, requiring all his concentration, yet he somehow made it home in one piece. He was exhausted; physically and mentally drained.

Dan toppled out of the driver's seat. The ground unexpectedly tilted to the right, and he took a couple of steps in that direction to keep his balance. Paul sprinted from the house, his eyes locked on Dan as he ran toward his brother.

"Dan! Are you all okay?" Paul looked at his twin, alarmed. "What happened to you?"

"A wall fell on me." Dan paused a second. "I think."

Paul gripped Dan's elbow as he hustled his brother into the dining room. He guided Dan to a chair and pushed his shoulder down so he was sitting upright. "Stay there," he commanded in a low, authoritative voice.

"Don't worry, I won't move." Dan groaned. "I'm not sure I can say the same about the room, though. You're my brother, right?"

"Yes." Paul left the room and returned with some bottles, bandages, and a wash cloth. He placed them on the table. "What happened?"

"Ahh...let me think...yeah, you're right...Ridgway is staying at the lake," Dan said as Paul brushed back the hair by his temple and began to clean away the blood. Dan half-rose out of the chair. "Ow! Ow!"

"Sit still." Paul pushed his brother down. "The antiseptic is going to sting worse than this. You'll grow a pretty bump there.

Swelling started already." He continued to work. "Keep talking."

"Okay...Ridgway walked up to the lodge. I followed but didn't see him anywhere. I thought I heard something from inside, and noticed the plywood had been moved from the back door," Dan said. "I went in, got to the living room, and pow! Blackout." He sucked in his breath and winced. "Ow! Have mercy! Stop! You're killing me here!"

"Cut out the whining. Let me get this bandage on," Paul huffed. "Did you lose consciousness?"

"Yeah. I think so...yeah, must have."

"How long were you out?" Paul asked as he finished up.

"Not very. A couple of minutes. Three or four. Maybe five." Dan reached up to touch the bandage on his head. Paul slapped his hand down.

"Hands off. Do you think Ridgway clobbered you?" Paul put the first aid items away.

"Who knows? I remember nothing after stepping into the living room," Dan said. "When I came to, I was under a pile of left-overs from a wall."

"So it could have been that Ridgway slugged you, then he pushed the wall over to cover up, or he shoved the wall on top of you," Paul said.

"Or he wasn't in there at all. The wall fell because it was damaged, and the weather over the years weakened it, and I was at precisely the wrong place at precisely the wrong time." Dan shrugged. "Pick a card, any card."

"We will leave those questions until tomorrow." Paul helped

Dan to his feet. "Right now, my dear brother, you're going to your bedroom and rest."

"Aw, gee, do I have to?" Dan asked like a little kid.

"Yes you do, young man," Paul replied in his best dad tone.

"Well, that may be a good idea. My head still hurts and things are a little woozy," Dan admitted as Paul guided him to his room. "Tell the room to stand still."

***

Dan woke in bed the next morning with just a slight headache. His brain seemed clear. He reached to touch the bandage.

"Ah, ah, ah. Leave it alone."

Paul's voice stopped Dan in mid-reach. Dan looked toward the source. Paul was in the desk chair, dressed in the same clothes he wore yesterday.

"Have you been there all night?" Dan asked.

Paul nodded.

Dan smiled gratefully at his brother, plumped the pillows and sat up in bed. "You're the best."

"And how is our little patient feeling this morning?" Paul asked.

"Our little patient is much better, thank you, doctor," Dan answered. "Very little headache, no spinning rooms. I appreciate the first aid treatment. Rough and ham-handed though it was."

"I'll take that as a compliment." Paul bowed his head in thanks. "It's in the job description. I am the eldest, after all."

"By two minutes," Dan scoffed.

"It still counts."

Dan chuckled. "Now my mind is clear and firing on all cylinders as usual—"

"Like a well-oiled Model T Ford." Paul sputtered like an old-time engine.

"Thank for your vote of confidence in my logical reasoning," Paul responded.

"Anytime. So what's the dope about Ridgway?"

"He is staying at the lake, under an assumed name. I mean, he isn't on the register." Dan waved toward his wallet and the list Donna gave him, resting on the bureau next to his tee-shirt. "Let me have that piece of paper, please." He continued after Paul passed it to him. "These are the current guests. I almost bumped into Ridgway outside Cottage Six, I think. Six or seven."

"Bumped into him!" Paul sat up straight.

Dan ran his finger down the column of names. "It was a near miss."

"Did he know it was you?"

"I don't think so." Dan shook his head, wincing a little at the throbbing that it had triggered. "I took off my tee-shirt, like I was going for a swim, and hid my face."

Paul nodded with approval. "That's cooking with gas."

Dan tapped a line on the paper. "Cottages Five and Seven are registered to couples. Here he is. Number six is Ward Wayigredd."

"That's a weird name," Paul commented.

"It most—wait a second...hold the phone." Dan stared at the name for a minute, then laughed. "Ward Wayigredd is an anagram for Edward Ridgway! Same letters, different order. You've got to give the man credit for creativity!"

"You weren't making much sense yesterday afternoon, but it sounded like you followed Ridgway to Wolf Lodge, correct?" Paul tented his fingers together as he listened.

"That's right. I trailed all the way up there, then lost sight of him," Dan related again. "I heard some noise from inside the building. I went in, and, well, the next thing I knew, my brain is bouncing around on the floor."

"And you remember nothing else?"

"Nope. Only...only...I think a saw something in the living room before I took my nap, but I just can't grab what from my memory." Dan sighed and leaned back on the pillows. "Let's take the whole thing in order, then perhaps we can figure out a clue on what is going on. That could prod my memory." Dan counted the items off on his fingers. "These are the things we know about our friend Eddie Ridgway. One, he left Chicago on a bus for Greenborough and slipped off at the Wayside Gas Station when the Greyhound took a rest stop but didn't get back on. Since he had the paid-for ticket in his possession, which I found, we can assume he wanted to miss the bus for an unknown reason."

"At least unknown to us," Paul said.

Dan nodded in agreement. "Two, he accepted a ride with us as far as Farmingford. After letting you out at the Epstein's house, I dropped him off at the auto court. He stayed there under his own name, and, according to Ted and the desk clerk, took the morning bus into Belmont, presumably to continue his journey to Greenborough. Does that sum it up?"

Paul raised his hand.

"We have a comment or question from the gentleman in the first row. Yes, sir?" Dan gestured toward Paul.

His brother stood. "In the interest of completeness, I wish to point out that we were passed by three vehicles after we turned on the highway. Two just before reaching the gas station, and one prior to getting to town." He sat again.

"So noted. The first was, if I remember, a blue sedan. Next was the bus and the third one was a black delivery van. Is that correct?" Dan looked at Paul, who nodded in agreement. "We know that the blue sedan belongs to Roy Archer, a private investigator representing the Worldwide Insurance Company. Obviously, Ridgway rode on the bus."

"What about the black van?" asked Paul.

"Let's see if we can figure out the reasons behind the earlier activities before we tackle that, and stick with the chronology." After thinking for a moment, Dan continued, "So does it make sense that Ridgway got off the bus at the Wayside because he knew Archer was on his tail?"

"I'd say so," Paul agreed.

Dan sat forward. "Ridgway knows he's being followed, so he left the bus at the rest stop and fooled Archer into believing that he boarded again. Archer trailed the bus to Belmont and discovered that Ridgway wasn't on it. That forced him to waste time backtracking all the way to the Wayside to pick up the trail again. Meanwhile, Ridgway scattered clues about traveling to Belmont, then actually did it. That gave him at least a half-a-day's lead over Archer, either to continue to Greenborough by bus or even switch to the train. Maybe not use the entire bus ticket and travel to a different location altogether."

"Why register at the auto court under his own name?" Paul wondered.

Dan shrugged. "Why not? Farmingford is small. Unless he slept under a bridge, there are only two places to stay in town. It wouldn't be difficult for Archer to check those out. That makes sense, except..."

"Both of us saw Ridgway at the lake," Paul finished. The two were quiet for a moment. "And there's something else we overlooked," he added in a glum tone.

"What have we overlooked?"

"A simple question," Paul said. "Why did Ridgway come back here?"

Dan flopped back on his bed and threw a pillow over his face. "Ah! We missed that one, didn't we? That reward money was too enticing, so we skipped the motive." He removed the pillow and drummed his fingers on the blanket. "It's possible he returned to throw Archer off the scent." He sighed. "No, that makes little sense. Why do that when he had the advantage of a head start?" He looked up at the ceiling as though expecting to find the answer there. "The only reason I could think of why Ridgway would come back to town is because—"

Dan sat up in bed, and the twins looked at each other. They spoke at the same time. "He hid the money around here."

Chapter Six

After a moment of enthusiasm, Dan shook his head. "No, that doesn't jibe."

"Why not?" Paul protested.

"Why not?" Dan threw up his hands. "Because why would Ridgway squirrel away his money in Farmingford, of all places? For what reason? How come here?"

"I don't know. Maybe he threw a dart at a map," Paul retorted. "We both saw him at the lake."

"Could be he likes trout fishing," Dan dismissed. "I don't know..."

"It is possible he hid the cash in the park," Paul persisted.

"You've got to be kidding! Glenstall Park is over twenty-five thousand acres!" Dan said. "And why there? Why not at Yosemite or stuff the money in the mouth of an alligator in the Everglades?" He growled in frustration. "The problem is we don't know enough to know what we don't know."

The two sat in a glum silence for a minute.

"Here's another odd thing," Paul said.

Dan spread his hands in resignation. "Go ahead. Dump it on the pile."

"It seemed Ridgway didn't care Archer located him again later," Paul noted.

Dan frowned. "Why do you say that?"

"Ken must have seen us give him a ride. He told Archer that. Ridgway may have wanted to make sure he had a witness. Then our passenger registered under his own name at the auto court, and then spread his sob story around about being sick and so on." Paul stood, walked to the window and looked out. "For somebody trying to be sneaky so he can scoop up his cash in secret, he scatters plenty of clues around, doesn't he?" Paul faced Dan. "He might as well stick a sign on his back saying 'follow me to the loot.'"

"True. Of course, it might have all been just a red herring for us to pass on to Archer if Archer caught up with us. To send him off in a different direction." Dan was quiet for a moment. "We need to deal with the practicalities first. Number one: how did he get back into town?"

"Perhaps he never took the bus in the first place," Paul suggested. "He could have done the fake boarding routine like he did before."

"I don't think so," Dan said. "The stop is in full view of the drugstore. Ted saw him get on and take a seat. Ridgway couldn't have hidden anywhere, unless he climbed out the window and jogged alongside the thing for a couple of blocks."

"Could he have hitchhiked? I mean, that's how we brought him into town," Paul asked.

Dan considered the idea for a moment, then shook his head. "Possible, but unreliable."

"All right." Paul ran his fingers through his brown hair. "How about this: he got off in Belmont, then grabbed the afternoon bus back here."

"That could be. Check that. The schedule is in the top drawer." Dan pointed toward his desk.

Paul pulled out the folded sheet of paper and examined the columns of printed numbers. He nodded. "It's a tight connection, but it could be done."

"Okay, that gets him to town, but how did he get out to the resort? There's no bus service out there," Dan said.

"That only leaves by car," Paul said, "so he had to get his hands on one. He's too smart to steal it, since that would cause a ruckus. The police would be on the lookout for a stolen vehicle."

"Perhaps a friend lent him one, or he bought one," Dan said.

"I'd take the borrow angle off the table," Paul said.

Dan raised his eyebrows in a question.

"He only talked about his non-existent brother in Omaha," Paul said. "Nobody else in Belmont or Greenborough."

"Let's hope there wasn't a friend in Belmont. If he borrowed a car, it would be difficult to trace," Dan said. "I agree with you. I vote for him buying a one. But how do we find out if he did?"

"There's only one way." Paul yanked the covers off Dan. "Your convalescence is now over. We'll shower and get ready, then visit Waxtons. Dibs on the bathroom first."

As Paul darted from the room, Dan called after him, "Don't use all the hot water!"

Paul stuck his head back in and gave an evil grin. "Cold showers are invigorating, my lad. Very healthy."

Dan leapt out of bed. "Which you'll find out when I get there ahead of you!" he challenged.

The wrestling race was on to see who would make it to the bathroom first. Dan did, although he thought Paul allowed it because of his injured state. After they showered and dressed, the twins scarfed down their breakfast. Dan dialed up Archer's office, leaving a request to call him back, and then clambered into the jeep with Paul. They drove off to Waxton's Wonderful Used Cars.

The lot took up a full block in Farmingford's small business district. A couple of dozen vehicles of all sorts were lined up in two rows, each windshield painted with the sales price along with slogans like "Like New!" and "A Steal!". The cars rested under strings of triangular red, white, and blue flags strung between the light poles. The only building stood at the back of the lot, no more than a shed, which served as the office. A sign over the door read: "Home of the Best Auto Deals in Town!" The sign failed to mention it was the home to the only auto deals in town.

Dan and Paul pulled into the parking lot and noticed Don Waxton, a jovial older man with a rounded belly, sitting on the porch of the office. His hair was going gray, and he was reclining in a chair with his feet up on the railing. "Greetings, lads!" he called out to them.

"Hi, Mr. Waxton!" the brothers answered as they climbed out of their jeep.

"Looking to trade in?" With a groan, Waxton took his feet off the railing and stood.

"No thanks, Mr. Waxton," Dan said as he and Paul reached the porch.

"Are you sure? I'll give you a good deal like before." Waxton winked. "My cars are getting mighty dirty."

The second-hand car dealer was very generous when negotiating on Dan and Paul's jeep, giving them a good deal because he wanted the vehicle off his lot. He even allowed them to pay the difference in price between their combined jobs' earnings and the cost of the purchase by washing his inventory for a couple of months.

Paul laughed. "No thanks, Mr. Waxton. The jeep suits us fine. We're just looking."

"Well, there's no charge to kick a few tires," Waxton said as he joined them.

The three of them meandered down the front line of cars, and the salesperson stayed true to his profession, touting the benefits of each vehicle they passed. "Ah, what do we have here? A 1941 Mercury Eight convertible. Just look at that shining red exterior! She's in superb condition and runs like a dream."

"And only driven by a little old lady to church on Sunday," Dan chided.

"Why, of course, son, of course! Just like all my inventory!" Waxton roared with laughter. "And this little baby will make you a hit with the girls!"

"Yeah, it sure would," Dan said. *I need more than a car to be a hit with the girls,* he thought ruefully.

As they walked along the next aisle, Paul seized the opportunity of a brief pause in Waxton's spiel.

"So how's business, Mr. Waxton?" he asked. "Sold anything recently? Like in the last couple of days? I notice some empty slots."

"Can't complain, son, can't complain," Waxton boomed. "I have had no sales in the last few days, though. But last week, why I moved—" The ringing of the phone cut Waxton off in mid-sentence. "Excuse me, boys. Go ahead and browse. You might find something and change your minds." Waxton bustled off to the office.

Dan and Paul glanced at each other with disappointment as they strolled past the line of automobiles. As they reached the final one, they waved to Waxton through the office window before making their way back to the jeep. Dan steered it around the corner and pulled into a spot on the curb.

"So much for Ridgway buying a car," Paul sighed. "Damn."

"It seems so." Dan pounded the steering wheel with his fists. "That blow to the head must have scrambled my brains! We're such dopes!"

"What do you mean, 'we'?"

"Yes, you and me. The plural pronoun," Dan returned. "We assumed Ridgway rode the bus back, then bought the car from Waxton. He could have easily picked up one in Belmont and driven to the lake. There are four or five auto lots up there, but we can't check each one of those." He was quiet for a moment before going on. "What I still can't figure out is Ridgway's connection with Farmingford, or the park. Honestly, if we could find that he had even some slight history with this town, like he'd known somebody who lived here, or had ever lived here himself or came here to hunt or fish or anything at all, that makes it easier to believe he stashed his loot here. Perhaps even give us some clues where to start looking."

Paul snapped his fingers. "What about the library? We can go there and see if we can uncover any information about him. That may help us with some pointers. It's worth a try, right?"

"That's not a bad idea, my dear brother, not a bad idea," Dan said, scratching his chin. "Let's go."

Dan and Paul drove to the Farmingford Public Library off Linden Avenue. A generous philanthropist had gifted it to the town back in the late 1800s, in an attempt to divert people's attention from his less-than-above-board business practices. Although its classical design always seemed too ornate and out of place in a rural farming area, Dan admired its grandeur, from the tall white columns to the intricate carvings decorating the capitals. Inside, magnificent wood paneling covered the reading room walls and a coffered ceiling, now marred by the unpleasant fluorescent lighting. Dan and Paul navigated through the aisles of books until descending to the basement that housed bound back issues of newspapers and magazines.

The attractiveness of the upstairs architecture did not reach down there; the underground room had the charm of a prison ward with cinder block walls painted in a dull institutional green. The area was musty and chilly despite the heat outside, and the cement floors were plain and cold. Somewhere one of the florescent lights, attached to a ceiling constructed from suspended sheets of sound-absorbing cardboard, buzzed like a trapped bee. The twins stood alone in front of the forest of bookcases.

Dan headed down an aisle, eyes scanning the gold lettering imprinted on the bindings of the thick tomes. "The Chicago papers might be a good place to begin," he said. "Rizzo met his end in 1929, and that's when Ridgway became a financial consultant. What name did he go by?"

"Ambrose something...ah, Dexter, that was it," Paul answered. "We're looking for Ambrose Dexter."

"He lasted six years before being found out, starting in 1929, so let's begin in 1935. Here's the *Chicago Tribune*." Dan grunted a little as he pulled the large, awkward book off the shelf. "It weighs more than I thought. I've got volume one."

"I'm right behind you with number two," Paul said.

The brothers set their burdens down on a nearby table with a loud thud and dragged up chairs. As the wooden legs scraped the concrete, they opened up the volumes and started combing through them in search of any information related to Ridgway or Dexter. Dan had to force himself to stay focused and ignore the other stories and advertisements from the past scattered along the pages.

After what felt like hours of searching through yellowed newspapers, at last Dan found a headline reading 'Local Investment Advisor Booked for Embezzlement'.

"Eureka! Get this!" Dan put his finger on the story and read out loud. "'Investment advisor Ambrose Dexter was arrested at his LaSalle Avenue office Thursday afternoon on charges of embezzlement. He is accused of skimming an undisclosed amount of money from the accounts of his clients over a span of six years.'"

"Three hundred thousand worth of undisclosed dollars," Paul added.

Dan nodded. "'The accounting irregularities'—that's a polite way to put it—'came to light when one client, the Superior Brewery Company on Fletcher Avenue—'" He glanced up at Paul and chuckled. "Once being involved with a bootlegger, it's tough to give up the liquor business, I guess."

Paul grinned. "Old habits die hard."

"You said it," Dan replied. He went back to the article. "Where was I? Ah...here '...Brewery Company on Fletcher Avenue requested an audit which uncovered a shortage of approximately thirty thousand dollars. In an unexpected twist, it was later discovered that Ambrose Dexter was in reality Edward Ridgway, long suspected of involvement with the Lorenzo Rizzo bootlegging operation.'"

Paul spoke like a huckster. "Get your illegal bootleg liquor from your pal, Lorenzo Rizzo. Only a dollar a bottle! Also a great spot remover!"

"Or stomach lining remover," Dan laughed. "Let's see...'Rival mobster Frankie McFarlane's men shot down Rizzo and fourteen of his gang members on June 23, 1929, effectively ending Rizzo's organization.'" He looked up at Paul. "Eighteenth anniversary of that minor event coming up." He went back to the story. "Ridgway disappeared after the massacre and was thought to have fled to South America. However, after a few months, he reemerged in Chicago as Ambrose Dexter. As Dexter, he managed the finances of one hundred different individuals, small companies and charities.”

“He stole from charities? What a creep,” Paul muttered. “Anything else?”

Dan skimmed the rest of the text. “That’s all the important stuff. The rest of the article is about how everybody was shocked that Ridgway—or Dexter—would do something like that.” He tapped the page. “Huh. Here’s a photo.”

The grainy picture was a harsh one, lit by a flash bulb, dividing the world into light and stark shadows. The policemen flanking Ridgway had stoic expressions, an expression of duty and responsibility on their faces. In contrast, the younger Ridgway smiled and appeared relaxed.

Paul leaned in for a closer examination. “Is that him? He doesn’t look the same.”

“That’s him all right,” Dan said. “You can tell by his facial features, the shape of his head...”

“From the perceptive eyes of the artist.”

Dan chuckled. “He was sporting a beard then and the hair style is different. They may be a different color, lighter than now, but I can’t tell with a black-and-white photo. He also looks fatter, more filled out.”

“I guess a decade in prison would thin a person. That would account for his paleness and how sickly he is,” Paul said.

“Remember that Archer said Ridgway’s a con man,” Dan countered. “Let’s see what else there is to find.”

They pored over the following editions and only found two

more stories. One that spoke of the fruitless search for the misappropriated funds and one that related how insurance companies, such as Worldwide, were paying claims knowing a crime had been committed.

Then the case dropped out of the news. The two continued the tedious task of checking more back issues, pulling volume after volume off the shelf. At one point, Paul laid on the table and pretended to perform a bench press using a stack of three of the weighty books.

The newspaper accounts resumed when the trial began several months later. The twins devoured the articles for details. Despite the ever-increasing mountain of evidence pointing to his conviction, Ridgway kept insisting that he was innocent but didn't mount much of a defense. In less than two days, the jury had reached a guilty verdict and sentenced Ridgway to prison. The vast fortune that he had stolen was nowhere to be found.

"Nothing about Farmingford, Belmont, or anyplace around here." Dan let the book fall shut.

"Let's check the *Record*. If Ridgway had some association with the town, it would have mentioned it. You know, a 'Local Boy Does Bad' type of story."

They put away the *Chicago Tribune*, replacing it with the *Farmingford Record* from the same era. The smaller newspaper was easier to search, but most of the stories were about dances, high school sports teams, and folks who took trips abroad. There was no mention of Ridgway.

Dan sat back in the chair and sighed. "That puts us back to

where we started. Why did Ridgway pick here to hide the money?"

"But we know for a fact that he's here, registered under a phony name in one of the cottages out at the lake." Paul pulled off his glasses and rubbed the bridge of his nose.

"Donna told me that the resort is fully reserved by March," Dan said. "His stay there isn't a spur-of-the-moment trip. He had to have planned it months in advance. And it doesn't seem likely he's here on a vacation."

Paul shrugged. "Maybe he's traveling incognito. He doesn't want anybody to recognize him. "

"That doesn't explain why he registered under his own name at the auto court. Perhaps he's dodging former members of the Rizzo gang." Dan dismissed the ideas with a wave. "Ah, this whole thing is getting too complicated. It may need a diagram." He stopped as a thought occurred to him. "The simplest answer is usually the best one. We may have been on to something when we thought Ridgway hid the money around here. Not knowing the why is annoying me. Let's turn this over a bit."

Paul linked his fingers behind his head as he thought. "Well, Ridgway is staying by the lake, and we both saw him head toward Wolf Lodge. Might as well—" He put a cautioning hand out. Leaning close to Dan, he whispered. "I think somebody is listening to us. Keep talking."

Dan continued, doing his best to make his conversation sound natural. He shuffled the newspaper books on the table with his hands to make more noise as he talked. "It's like they intended this money for a purpose, but then something must have gone wrong because it never reached its destination."

Paul rose from his chair, his gaze taking in the room, taking in every nook and cranny. He paced the floor of the basement cautiously. Dan also heard what his brother did: a slight shuffle of feet. Paul slipped out of sight behind a row of bookcases.

The overhead lights snapped off, plunging the room into darkness.

Chapter Seven

D an sat, straining to keep track of his brother's location in the pitch black. There came a muffled scuffle, a grunt from Paul, and then footsteps as someone raced up the concrete stairs. The basement door flew open and slammed shut, a shaft of light slicing into the blackness. Another person repeated the performance, running upstairs and out of the basement. Everything went quiet.

I can't just sit here alone in the dark, Dan thought. Pushing himself to his feet, he held his arms out before him as he aimed toward the stairs, stumbling through the darkness, hoping he didn't run into another unknown visitor. He fanned his fingers through the air, left and right, high and low, and encountered the cool, smooth wooden top of a second table. He moved around it and misjudged its size; a fact he discovered when his thigh crashed into a sharp corner.

"Damn!" He rubbed his leg.

He continued to play blind-man's bluff across the room until he collided with a heavy bookshelf. Placing one hand on a shelf and holding the other one in front of him, he guided himself toward the stairs, until finally grasping the cold metal of the banister. He transferred both hands to it, then reached out to fumble for the switches.

"Where are they?" Dan grumbled to himself. "They should be at the bottom of the stairs."

It took several attempts, but he found them at last and flipped them up. The lights flickered on with a hum, illuminating the basement. He was alone, so Paul must have been one of the people who dashed up the steps. Dan climbed to the first floor and hurried through the library, casting glances around him as he searched for his brother. He discovered him on the outside porch.

"Don't ask because, no, I didn't see who it was," Paul told Dan as he walked up. "I figured out where he was and was inching around the edge of one shelf when whoever it was doused the lights. The switches are right there. We grappled for a bit, then mystery man broke free, delivered a solid whack on my skull with a book and then took off."

"Do you think it was Ridgway?" Dan asked.

"Who knows?" Paul shrugged. "With those lights out, it was too dark to see anything."

"It might have been Ridgway. If he conked me over the head at the lodge, he may want to know how much we know." Dan leaned against a pillar, arms folded. "But I'm not positive he did that."

"It could be another investigator is out after the reward," Paul suggested. "Some freelancer following Archer. He saw him talk to us, so maybe he's trailing us now."

"That's possible, I suppose, but I'm skeptical," Dan said. "If it was, he's not the model of a professional detective. Why didn't he just act like Richards and tell us who he was? Why lurk in the basement like the phantom of the library?"

"Perhaps the guy isn't on the up and up," Paul said. "You know, a private eye that's a little shady."

Dan moved away from the pillar and spread his hands. "Why mess with us? What does he gain from it? Unless he's grasping for any information at all because he's as much in the dark as we are." He shot a glance at Paul. "No, that was not meant as a pun."

"Good."

"The lake and Wolf Lodge are the only constants we have so far in the business," Dan said after a moment's thought, "and whoever Mr. Big Ears was heard us talking about it."

"Do you think he's on his way out there now?"

"It seems likely. Wouldn't you?"

"You bet I would." Paul made a sweeping gesture toward their jeep. "So off we go?"

"Off we go," Dan confirmed. "Perhaps we'll meet our library friend in the bright sunshine of the day."

The two drove to the park, Dan at the wheel. Before they reached the main entrance, he quickly swerved off the highway onto a narrow dirt road that led to one of their fishing spots.

Paul grabbed onto the windshield to brace himself. "Jeez! Warn a guy when you're about to do something like that."

"Sorry. I just had a sudden thought."

"And that triggered a sudden turn?"

"I realized that Mr. Big Ears knows what we look like, but we don't know what he looks like. He's unknown to us," Dan explained as he slowed the jeep. "That gives him quite an advantage. If we parked in the main lot and walked up to the lodge, he could spot us, but we wouldn't know it. I figure we could park by the quarry and hike to the lodge from the opposite side. It's not far."

Paul gave a single nod of his head, and Dan eased the jeep into a lower gear. The vehicle jostled along the bumpy road riddled with potholes and lined with thickly packed trees and bushes that seemed to reach out to grab at them as they passed. Several narrow roads split off from the main one, some barely recognizable as such among the dense forest.

Dan slowed down to navigate around the wider tree trunks as they wound up a series of tight switchbacks toward the top of the ridge. The terrain grew steeper and rougher with each turn until it finally leveled out on top where the road ended in a jumble of enormous boulders.

The jeep rumbled to a stop, and Dan switched off the engine. The brothers climbed out, squinting in the bright sun. To the left was the quarry—a good-sized crater carved into the terrain with steep walls at least thirty feet high, sloping down to a flat, empty bottom littered with sharp stones. A small metal shed stood against the far cliff face. To their right, a dirt trail wound down towards the lake and one of their favorite fishing spots.

The brothers skirted the massive boulders and continued on what used to be the road, now reduced to an indistinct path, occasionally blocked by fallen trees or bushes that had grown wild over the years. After a few minutes of pushing their way through the woods, they emerged on a well-maintained trail that cut through dense greenery. Finally, their destination came into view: the lodge's charred remains, looming like an eerie apparition against a stunning backdrop of glimmering blue water and lush green hills.

Two small children, a girl and a boy, broke the silence with their happy shouts and laughter ringing out as they ran around in circles on the porch. Their parents stood with their backs to Dan and Paul, taking in the peaceful, serene landscape.

Paul leaned into Dan and whispered, "At least with these people here, Ridgway or our unknown visitor can't do anything which draws attention to themselves."

The twins strolled toward the lodge, their feet shuffling along the dirt. When the family started back down the drive in the resort's direction, Dan turned to Paul and gave a subtle nod. The two headed toward the back corner of the building

Dan surveyed their surroundings one last time, making sure no one was watching, before yanking back the heavy plywood sheet which blocked the kitchen door. He held it open for his brother and motioned for Paul to enter first, and followed. Dan snugged the wood over the doorway again.

"Should we search the place?" Paul asked in a quiet voice. "Ridgway could have been looking for a secret compartment or niche downstairs. Perhaps something under the floorboards."

"It would take some time to check everything, even with what's left of this place. There could be dozens of spots to stash things." Dan looked around. "Keep an eye out for anything that seems disturbed, anyway. Areas where the dirt and leaves have been brushed away, stuff like that. That could hint at a hiding place. Right now, though, we need to find some clue putting Ridgway inside this lodge." Dan pointed. "Let's check the second floor. I didn't make up there the last time."

They walked through the dining room and into the hall, starting upstairs. They took one step at a time, the wooden treads creaking under their combined weight. They stopped when they reached the top because they could go no farther. The second floor over the living room had been totally burned, reduced to blackened perimeter walls that protruded from the remains like charred bones.

"Brief trip," Dan remarked as he glanced around. "If Ridgway hid anything up here, it's nothing but charcoal now."

The brothers checked the other two rooms remaining over the kitchen and dining room. They were covered in debris, leaves and dirt deposited through the open roof.

Dan shrugged, "Nothing here. Let's go back downstairs. Maybe that will help me remember what I saw before I was conked out."

The two went back down the creaking staircase and entered the living room. Paul noticed the rubble on the floor and gave a whistle. "You were under all that, Dan?"

"Yep. It was a very snug fit."

"You're lucky you only got a bump on the head with all that stuff on top of you." Paul poked at the pile of splintered wood with the toe of his shoe.

"Don't I know it, brother." Dan strode to the center of the

room, scanning the area. He planted his fists on his hips and muttered, "By the fireplace." His gaze landed on something on the stone hearth. He rushed over and seized it.

"What have you got there?" Paul came up next to Dan.

"A new pencil..." Dan read the lettering on the shaft. "...a number 2B."

"Anything important about that?"

"A 2B has soft lead and is darker...easier to erase." Dan said. "Artists use them for sketching. I have a bunch. Let's see if I can..." He closed his eyes and concentrated. "Wait...wait...I remember...it's coming back...yes, yes, a pencil was lying on the...by the..." He opened his eyes and pointed at Paul. "That's it! Before someone or something knocked me out, I saw an open creel, with some paper in it, in front of the fireplace. A pencil was on the floor right next to it."

"That pencil?" Paul nodded toward it.

"*A* pencil, but it could have been this one." Dan examined it. "It looks brand new. If it had been inside here for any time, it would be as dirty as everything else."

"So what's Ridgway doing in the lodge with a pencil?" Paul arched one eyebrow. "Do you have a competitor in the local art market?"

Dan looked around the room and shrugged. "Who knows? There's not much left to draw. Maybe he has an artistic side, and he likes ruins."

"Like another artist I know." Paul cast a sidelong glance at this twin.

"Shut up, you cretin," Dan said. "But if he used this pencil, his fingerprints would be all over it. It would be more evidence to provide to Richards. Do you have a handkerchief?"

"Only a tissue." Paul pulled one from his pocket and gave it to his brother.

Dan wrapped the tissue around the pencil, then slipped it into his back pocket. "They always do that in the movies."

"You're a regular Sam Spade," Paul grinned. "Nothing else to see at the scene of the crime?"

Dan shook his head in resigned agreement and turned to leave, leading the way outside. After Paul stepped out, Dan replaced the plywood over the door and brushed off his hands. As he turned, the padlock hanging from the door of the small outbuilding caught his attention. He squinted and pointed at it, turning towards his brother. "The lock doesn't look right, does it?"

Paul peered at it. "No, it doesn't."

The two walked toward the door, and Dan crouched to examine the lock. He ran his fingers over the fresh cut in the hasp. Someone had sliced it just above where it would fit into the lock body, and twisted it back until it looked like it was still intact. With a swift tug, Dan removed the padlock, dropped it to the dirt, and opened the door. They both looked into the darkness inside.

Light squeezing through the narrow slit of a window high on the wall, bouncing off the corrugated metal roof, did little to dispel the gloom from the interior of the tiny building. The doorway was narrow. Dan pulled the door open and they stepped in.

The outbuilding held a little chill inside, and it took a moment for their eyes to become accustomed to the shadows. The tangy smell of pitch filled their nostrils, and the long-exposed beams exuded a pungent odor of age that had seeped into the wood.

"This shed must have been for the well. There's the equipment." Dan pointed. In the distant corner of the room a corroded water pump was still identifiable next to an aged gasoline motor.

Paul whispered, "Look, by the pump. Isn't that a cash box?"

A black metal box lay on the floor. The lid was open, revealing little more than emptiness.

"Ridgway must have been here already," Dan said. "We were wrong. He hid the money in this building, not inside the lodge. He's already cleaned out the till and recovered the loot."

The brothers walked slowly through the doorway, their eyes glued to the box sitting on the far side. As they reached the middle of the room, a loud creaking sound rose, as if the floorboards were groaning beneath them. The boys stopped in place and a chill rippled through them as they realized what was happening. Dan and Paul exchanged frightened glances.

"Let's get out of here!" Paul yelled.

The wooden planks of the floor vibrated and shifted like a gentle wave. As the brothers turned to flee, the crunching of splintering timber filled the air. The floor under them gave way, and they plummeted into the blackness below.

Chapter Eight

They dropped swiftly, clutching at the air as they plummeted downwards until they splashed into water, their skin burning as the icy temperature seeped into their bones. Thrashing in a frantic battle to keep their heads above the surface, coughing and spluttering, they gulped for breath. Finally, they got themselves under control by treading water.

Paul spoke up, "Are you all right?"

"Yeah," Dan replied. "You?"

"Okay."

"Where are we?"

"We must be at the bottom of the lodge's well." Paul spat out some more water.

Dan grabbed one stone protruding from the wall. "Hang on to these rocks. They'll hold us up so that we won't tread water and get tired."

Paul found a rock and steadied himself. "Well, at least we didn't fall into the cesspool."

"That's what I like about you," Dan said. "You always look on the bright side."

"This thing must be deep." Paul looked down. "I never touched bottom."

"Me neither." Dan shivered, not only from the cold temperature of the water. With a little difficulty, he kept his tone level. "Okay, okay, let's figure out how to get out of here."

"Yeah, right. Like Miss Johnson used to say in first grade: 'time to put our thinking caps on.'" Paul gave a weak, unconvincing laugh.

For a few long minutes, their prison was silent, the only sound being their breathing and the gentle lap of water against the stone walls. Dan looked around, gazing at the circle of rough rocks which enclosed the two. They reached up about eight feet over his head, slippery with a coating of slime. The well measured five or six feet in diameter. A noise came from up top, like footsteps.

"Listen! Somebody is up there!" Dan shouted. "Hey! Hello! Help! We're down here! Help! We need help!"

Paul and Dan's voices rose in a deafening chorus, echoing off the sides of the well. Dan caught sight of a figure lurking in the shadows beyond the edge of the well. He was sure someone was there, watching them.

"He's seen us!" Dan exclaimed as he waved his free arm. "Down here! We're down here! Help!"

The figure's silhouette quickly vanished, and the boys heard the door to the building open and close. A heavy silence engulfed them as fear, anger, and disbelief settled in. Dan and Paul shook with rage, their curses filling the round chamber and bouncing off its walls.

"If I ever get my hands on that guy, he's going to wish he was never born. Fine, so be it. We have to find our own way out. There is only one way: up." Paul surveyed the wall, his brow furrowed in determination. He reached up and grasped a rock. His biceps bulging with effort, gritting his teeth, he heaved himself up onto the slippery surface. The slime covering the stones caused his grip to falter, and he tumbled back into the liquid below. Resurfacing, he spat out some water. "That goop has made the rocks slick."

"We can't get out of this place like that," Dan said.

"Well, we can't stay here forever," Paul snapped. "Any bright ideas?"

"Not right now."

"That's not very helpful," Paul grumbled.

"Well, if I come up with an idea, I'll make sure you'll be the first to know," Dan fired back. He took a second to think. "What about this? Can you hang against the wall and let me climb on your shoulders?"

"It's worth a shot." Paul checked around until he found a crevice and dug his fingers into it. "Hop aboard."

Dan grabbed Paul's shoulders and pulled himself up inch by inch up his brother's back. Paul's body shook as he clung to the slimy stone, his knuckles turning white with effort.

"No way!" Paul panted. "I'm—"

But he didn't even have time to finish his sentence before he lost his grip, and Dan's weight shoved him under the water. It felt like an eternity before Dan yanked his brother back to the surface. Both of them held onto the wall, coughing and gasping.

"No good. I wasn't even halfway up," Dan said. "Strike one."

They were quiet again, then Paul broke the silence. "Come on. Same idea, different approach. I'll make a cradle for your foot. I'll give you a boost while you jump."

"You're going underwater when I lunge," Dan cautioned.

"That's okay," Paul said. "I'll tell you when. I'll be ready."

Paul laced his fingers together, forming a cup as he tread water. Dan put one foot into the cradle of Paul's hands. After taking a deep breath and holding it, Paul lifted. Dan's body rose as he pushed up with his leg while he reached out desperately for something to hold on to. His hands kept sliding off the rocks, and he dropped back with a large splash. The two gripped to the wall to keep them from slipping back under the surface.

"Strike two," Dan said under his breath.

"We can't hang on to these walls forever!" Paul spat out. "We're going to die by drowning or starvation, like rats!"

"Tell me something I don't know!" Dan shouted back.

"Well, come up with something, you paint pusher!"

"Don't you think I'm trying, you dumb boxer?" Dan yelled.

"Why you—" Paul's fists clenched around the rock as his anger boiled over. He let go of the stone to take a swing at Dan. His brother ducked, and responded by putting one knee in Paul's chest and pushing him back. Paul's body floundered in the water, his feet brushing the other side of the shaft before he pulled them away. He motioned to Dan. "Hold on, hold on! I've got an idea! Wait! Let me try something!"

Paul pushed his shoes onto the wall opposite him, put out his arms, pressing tight to the stones on each side. He followed that by jamming his shoulders and upper back against the jagged rocks. With every muscle shaking, he inched his way up the steep sides, sliding one foot up and then the other, then hunched his shoulders and moved his hands higher. His breath came out in short bursts as he clenched his teeth together, focusing all of his energy on scaling up the shaft.

"You can do it!" Dan encouraged. "Move your feet up a bit—one at a time!"

Paul continued, working himself upward, his body strained against the tight walls as he hoisted his body up inch by inch. Veins bulged on his neck and arms, groans of effort escaped from his throat. He moved his feet up, followed by his shoulders and hands, until he came out of the water. He stopped, panting from exertion, looked at Dan and managed a grin. "So, who's the dumb boxer now?"

"Nobody I know! Keep going, buddy, you're doing great!" Dan said.

Gasping for breath, he continued for a few precious inches, before he cried out, "I'm never going to reach the top at this rate. It's too far away. It will take forever to reach it. I don't have the energy. I guess this is strike three."

Dan's words had a trace of despair in them as he said, "No, we can't give up now. We must try something—there's no other option." A thought came to him. "Can you hold that position?"

"It's not comfortable, but I'm stuck in here pretty good."

"Can you support my weight like that?"

Paul glanced at his brother. "I'm not sure. What's the idea?"

"Let me try to stand on you so I can reach up there," Dan said, "like a scaffold."

"Okay, but make it snappy." Paul sounded dubious.

"Ready?"

"As ready as I'll ever be." Paul wedged himself in the shaft, his arms, legs, and shoulders braced against the walls as tightly as he could. Every muscle trembled as Dan laid his arms over Paul's legs. Carefully and cautiously, Dan pulled himself out of the water, climbing onto his brother's torso. He worked with deliberate slowness, knowing that the slightest wrong motion could send Paul plunging down, wincing every time Paul let out a groan. Minutes passed until Dan got both knees up.

"Are you okay? Can you hang on?" Dan asked, in a combination of fear and anticipation.

"No, I'm–"

Paul slipped off the wall, and the two dunked back into the water. They grabbed each other and kicked toward the surface. Spitting out water, the two clung to the rocks.

"Fresh spring water. Bah!" Dan said. "That's it, buddy. Now it's strike three."

They were silent for a moment.

"No, my dear brother, this game is going into extra innings," Paul declared. "We can try the cradle again."

Dan shook his head. "It's no use. The top was feet above my head."

"Okay, climb up my back again—"

"That won't work. It didn't before."

"Not the way we did it. We need to take care of the slime. Give me hand." With Dan's help, he yanked off his tee-shirt, soaked it in the water, then used it to wash down the stones. He tossed garment over his shoulder and pressed his hands into the unforgiving stone until his fingers found a tight crevice. "There! I've got a good grip–I think. Let me get me feet set..." His legs churned beneath him as he fought for a foothold. "Got it. Okay, climb up my back."

"Paul, no. Why? It didn't–"

"Don't argue with me!" Paul yelled. "I can't hang around all day!"

"Very funny," Dan muttered as he grabbed Paul's shoulders. He hauled himself up his brother's back with guttural grunts, pulling himself inch by inch up. Every muscle in Paul's body shook as he fought to keep his grip on the stone, his fingers turning an almost translucent white. "How are you doing, buddy? Can you hang on?"

"Not long." Paul's voice was strained and graveled with pain.

Dan got his knees on Paul's shoulders, then got to his feet, stretching his arms out to their full length but feeling his fingers still a foot away from the edge of the well. Paul quivered beneath him, his body rigid as iron cables, ready to snap at any moment. "I have to jump for it, Paul. It will force you back down."

Paul just sighed, a sound of agony and firmness combined, and uttered a simple phrase: "Shut up and do it!"

Dan knew this was his only chance. Paul had no more strength left for a second try. Dropping into a deep crouch, he sprung upward with all the power he could muster. He heard a loud cry and the splash of Paul hitting the water as Dan dug at the wall with his hands, finally getting a hold, his body hanging full length down the shaft. "Paul?"

"I'm okay. Keep going!" Paul said.

His muscles burned as Dan forced his fingers between the cracks of rock and hauled himself higher towards the edge. His toes clawed frantically, trying to find a purchase, while his strained arms felt like they were being ripped from his shoulders.

"Go Dan, go! You're almost there!" Paul yelled from below. "You've got to do it! You're our only hope!"

"Great, no pressure," Dan forced out through a clenched jaw.

With every bit of strength he could summon, Dan struggled to make the top. At last, he hooked his chin onto the stones at the rim of the shaft as he gritted his teeth and fought to lift his weight up. With a last surge of energy, he heaved himself out of the well and flopped onto the floor above. He rolled over on his back, overcome by exhaustion but laughing that he had succeeded.

"Oh, Dan!" came a lilting cry from down in the well. "Don't forget your dear brother down here!"

"Wait! Let me see if I can find a rope or something." Dan got to his feet, peered over the lip and wagged a finger. "Now don't go anywhere."

"I wouldn't dream of it."

Dan took a quick glance around the room, but there was no rope. He returned to the well. "There's nothing here that I can use to help you. I'm going to the resort to get help. Can you hang on until I come back?"

Paul's voice echoed back. "What choice do I have? Just hurry!"

"On my way! Won't take me more than—" Dan reached the door and pulled. It didn't move. He tugged at the doorknob a few more times, then bent over to peer through the cracks.

"What's up, Dan?"

"Remember that shadow...that figure who was here before?"

"Yeah."

"That jerk shut the door and replaced the padlock," Dan pounded his fist on the metal surface and yelled. "Hey! Is anyone out there? Can you hear me?"

He peeked through the boards again. The area outside the shed was empty of people. "Great! Where are those tourists when you need them?" In a fit of frustration, he shook the door some more. "Hang on, Paul. I need to come up with something." Suddenly, his face lit up with an idea and he stripped off his shirt. "Paul, throw your shirt up here."

"Here it comes!"

Dan retrieved the soggy tee-shirt as it popped above the lip of the hole. He rolled his and Paul's garments tightly, then tied them end-to-end, creating a cloth rope about three and a half feet long. He got down on the ground. "This is supposed to work with bedsheets." He took hold of one end of the makeshift rope and lowered it into the shaft his arms' length. "Can you grab the end?"

The answer came as a powerful force yanked downward on Dan. Paul was clambering up the rope of tee-shirts, gasping, his feet slipping against the slippery rock wall.

"Hurry! It's slipping out of my grip!" Dan gasped out.

When Paul got close enough, Dan seized his brother's forearm. Paul released the tee-shirts and clung to the lip of the well with one hand, then with the other, fighting to pull himself out. Dan, tossing the knotted tee-shirts over his shoulder, snagged Paul's belt and tugged with all his might. In a final thrashing struggle, Dan pulled Paul over the lip. They both tumbled onto the ground, exhausted.

"Thanks," Paul said after he caught his breath. "Now I know who to call the next time I fall down a well."

Dan laughed. "Anytime, my dear brother, anytime."

"Also, remind me to write a commendation letter to the company that made those tee-shirts. They could use the testimonial in an ad." Paul sat up. "It was stupid for us to walk across rotten floorboards."

"They weren't rotten." Dan also sat up and pointed. "Look at the jousts at the edge of the well. They're not jagged, like a break."

"They're smooth," Paul said. "That meant somebody—"

"Stuck a saw between the floorboards and cut the joists almost all the way through. We stepped on that section and down we went."

"A booby trap," Paul whispered.

"A very well planned one," Dan said. "The bait was that cash box—" He glanced to where it had lain. It was gone. "Whoever did this wanted to get rid of us and the evidence. Somebody who knew we were coming out here."

"Mr. Big Ears?"

"Likely, but we still don't know who that was," Dan responded. "You couldn't be sure it was Ridgway who socked you at the library. It may have been the other detective on the case, if there is one. We don't even know if we were the intended victims of this trap. Ridgway could have set it for us or for Mr. Big Ears. Mr. Big Ears could have wanted Ridgway to fall into it. And so on and so on."

"Well, we have the pencil, at least. That has fingerprints on it, so…" Paul stopped when he saw the expression on Dan's face. "You do have the pencil, don't you?"

Dan patted himself down. He gave a weak smile and pointed down the well.

"Ah, this whole thing gives me a headache," Paul growled. "Let's get out of here, even if that means we take this place apart, piece by piece!"

Standing, Paul paced the perimeter of the shack's walls. "No way through stone walls." He stopped to check the narrow ventilation slot by the engine. "Too narrow," he muttered to himself, then stamped the planks underfoot to check the floor for weaknesses. "Too close to the ground anyway," he sighed. "They don't make them like they used to, which is bad news for us. Everything seems pretty tight," he announced.

His eyes fell on the door. "Let me try a more direct approach," Paul said with grim determination. He rushed forward and threw all of his weight against the door, clenching his fists and firing his shoulder like a cannonball. Even with all his might, the door still refused to budge, the padlock's rattle giving a mocking response. Paul winced, rubbing his shoulder. "That thing's not budging without a fight."

Dan stood. "The roof, Paul. That may be our way out."

His brother looked up. "You're right! The roof's just corrugated metal sheets nailed down to two-by-four rafters. If we could pry up a couple of those panels..." He attempted to touch one. "I can barely get to it."

"Come over here to the wall." Dan bent down, placing his elbows on his knees for support. "This time you can climb on me. I'll give up you a piggyback ride so you can get nearer to the roof. Do you think that would work?"

"A breeze!" Paul said. "Stand still, now. Here comes a hundred plus pounds of pure muscle!" He clambered onto his brother's bent back, wrapping his legs around his chest. Dan stood as Paul balanced himself with his hands on the wall. He stretched upward to the roof and rapped on the metal. "That's it! I've got plenty of leverage this way!"

The two inched along the sides of the shack, Paul straddling Dan to form a human ladder as they sought a way out. After about five minutes of searching, near the edge of the roof far from the door, Paul spoke. "Here's a likely one. A corner is curling." With a grunt, he pushed with all his might and the nails squeaked in protest as they were ripped loose.

"Heave, Paul!" Dan yelled. "Heave ho!"

Paul exerted upward pressure. The end of the metal sheet released its hold of the joist with a harsh groan of rusty nails. Welcome sunlight streamed through the crack.

"That's one corner," Paul called down to his brother. "Work backwards a little so I can get the other side."

Dan slowly backed his way about half a foot, with his brother straddling him. Paul forced the corrugated metal up all along its length until the panel snapped open at the other end.

Both boys whooped in triumph as the section was wrenched free to fall outside. Paul hopped down.

"C'mon, buddy! Your turn," Paul panted, grasping Dan around the knees and hoisting him.

Dan reached his hands up, gripped the edges of the opening, and pushed his body up. His feet scraped at the side of the other rafters. Sweat beaded his forehead. He thrust his body higher, wringing with every ounce of strength from his tired arms.

He pulled his legs up and through the opening, swung his knees forward and up to hook his toes on the edge of the long narrow hole. With much grunting, scraping, and exhaling, he struggled through onto the shed roof. Dan slid to the edge and hung by his hands to avoid any chance of injuring his legs by jumping to the ground, then lowered himself down to the dirt. Jogging to the front of the building, he took off the lock and opened the door wide.

"Exit this way, if you please." Dan performed a low bow as he held his one arm out from his side.

"Last time I stay at this dump," Paul said as he walked by, the tee-shirt rope dangling from one hand.

"I'll take your concerns up with management." Dan swung the door closed and slipped the lock back on. He pulled off his wet shoes and socks and stuffed his socks in his shoes.

"Two death-defying escapes in one day," Paul said as he untied the shirts. He handed one to his brother. "That may be a record."

Dan took his wet tee-shirt and wrung it out. "Yeah, but I wonder what the limit is."

Chapter Nine

Dan and Paul trudged back to the jeep in silence. Dan was mulling over what they had gone through. It seemed like something was off, as though an invisible piece of the puzzle was missing. But before he could put everything together, Paul jumped into the driver's seat and prepared to start the engine.

"Dan!" a girl's voice called. "Paul!"

Dan turned around. Donna, dressed in her work uniform, came up to them. He attempted to straighten his disordered clothing.

Donna smiled. "What happened? You two are soaking wet!"

"We fell into—" Paul started.

"The lake," Dan finished with a warning glance toward his brother.

"With your clothes on?" Donna asked.

"Well, we were horse playing, and, well, you know..." Dan's voice trailed off.

Donna folded her arms and laughed. "Boys will be boys!"

Dan awkwardly joined in the laughter. "Yeah."

"All right, both of you. Let's dry your clothes." Donna clapped her hands like a kindergarten teacher. "Housekeeping should be done for the day. We'll use their dryer."

"But—" Dan began.

"You'll catch a cold in those wet clothes, even in this heat." She waved her hand toward the resort and gave a playful tug on Dan's arm. "Come on, don't be stubborn."

"I won't," Dan meekly replied. He heard a snicker behind him, and he snapped his head toward his brother. Paul was climbing out of the jeep, grinning. Dan pointed and mouthed, "You shut up."

"I'll get the key." Donna waved a hand toward the resort. "The laundry is behind the office. Meet me there." She walked quickly ahead and disappeared around the corner of a building.

Paul fell into step. As they approached the cottages, Dan turned to Paul. "Keep an eye out for Ridgway," he whispered. He tilted his head toward Cottage 6. The curtains were still closed. "That's his room."

Paul nodded.

Donna stepped out from behind the next cluster of cabins and beckoned to them. "Hey, boys! Over here!"

The brothers waved back and hurried over. Donna led them through an open door, and into the small room, filled with the fresh smell of clean laundry and the dusty, sweet aroma of detergent. Shelves lined the walls, piled with sheets, pillowcases, and towels, all folded in orderly stacks like rows of linen soldiers. A commercial washer and dryer stood against one wall.

Donna went to the dryer and twisted a few knobs. "Take off your clothes and put them in here. Push the red button. Shoes outside," she directed as she pulled two towels off a shelf. She handed them to Dan and Paul. "You can wear these while you wait. Don't worry. Nobody will come in. It should only take about twenty minutes to dry your stuff. I've got to go to work. I'll check back later."

"Thanks a lot, Donna," Dan said.

"Anytime, handsome." Donna smiled and left the room, and with a finger-twiddling wave, closed the door.

Paul gave a low, throaty growl.

Dan swung around and planted a fist on Paul's shoulder. "I'm never going to hear the end of this, am I?"

Paul laughed. "Not in your lifetime...handsome."

"How did I ever got stuck with you as a brother..." Dan complained as he undressed.

"You're just lucky, I guess."

"I bet I did something horrible in a previous life." Dan tossed his clothes into the tub and toweled himself off. "Yeah, that must be it. And you're my punishment."

"The way I figure it, you did something wonderful in a past life. I'm your reward." Paul added his clothes to the drum. He dried himself and snapped his towel at Dan.

"Ouch!" Dan returned the favor, then wrapped his towel around his waist. "Push the button, dope."

Paul started the cycle, while Dan slipped their shoes outside in the sun. Back inside, Dan hopped on a counter next to Paul to wait as the dryer rumbled.

"Something is bothering me," Dan spoke after a pause.

"I'm sure you're going to tell me."

Dan tapped each word out on the counter. "Why is Ridgway

here?"

"To pick up the loot," Paul answered. "We've decided that."

"No, no. What I meant was, why is he *still* here?" Dan ran his fingers through his hair. "He's been in the area for what, three days now?"

"About that long. So what?"

"So why hasn't he grabbed the money and split? Why is he hanging around?" Dan shrugged. "Is he taking a vacation in celebration?"

"Not if he realizes he's being tailed," Paul said. "And we think he does, certainly by Archer, at least."

"That's it. People are on his heels. He knows that. One, or possibly two detectives, depending on who Mr. Big Ears was. Ridgway should have vamoosed as soon as he glommed onto the cash, winging his way down Mexico way by now." Dan drummed his fingers as he thought. "But he's still here."

"So what do you think it means, Sherlock?"

Dan didn't answer for a moment, then he faced Paul. "It means something must have gone wrong. Something's stopping him from collecting the stash."

"Or someone," Paul added.

"Or someone," Dan agreed.

"Maybe he's waiting for Archer to give up," Dan said.

Dan shook his head. "I think Ridgway understands that's not likely."

"Okay. Where does Wolf Lodge fit in?" Paul asked.

"What about it?"

"That always seems to be his destination. Let's say he hid the money inside but didn't count on the place burning down." Paul jerked his thumb toward the lodge. "He's poking around in the hopes to find at least a little something among the ashes. That's what is taking so long."

Dan thought about it. "Wolf Lodge was owned by somebody, until the state took it four years ago to add to the park. That's when the historical society paid me to do the sketches and photos of the interior. It was vacant for years earlier. But why pick the lodge? What's his connection to it? Who knows?" He shrugged. "Besides, I think Ridgway's too smart to cache loot on a random piece of private property. That would complicate retrieving the money. A house may be occupied, and he'd have to risk breaking into it. Or if he tried some abandoned building instead, that might be torn down before he could return. Not to mention the possibility of a fire."

"Forget the building, then. How about the land, then?" Paul said. "The lodge sits on a lot of ground, doesn't it?"

"Acres and acres. Hundreds, I think." Dan got off the counter and paced. "You stumbled onto something, my dear brother. Let's pretend Ridgway decided to go the Long John Silver route, and buried the cash in...oh, I don't know, let's say, in a farmer's field somewhere. Problem: that patch of ground might be dug up any day, either uncovering the money or slicing it to ribbons with a plow or something. A vacant piece of land could be cut, cleared, or even built on. Presto! His loot is under a concrete foundation." He stared out the window and waved one hand at the view. "So, as much as I hate to admit it, you were right yesterday.”

“He said I’m right! I’m going to circle this day on my calendar!” Paul laughed. “Correct about what, pray tell?”

“Your idea of using a heavily wooded state park to hide something. Most of the land is left in its natural state. I mean, that’s the point.” Dan turned to Paul. “So, if I were Ridgway and seeking a safe spot to stash the cash—”

“Nice alliteration.”

“Thank you. So, let us deduce where exactly that would that be.” Dan considered this for a moment. “We know he’s intelligent, so he would choose a place that would be difficult for the cops to find, and he could reasonably assume he’d always have access. It must be somewhere with plenty of cover and out of the way from prying eyes. This is where you’re correct. Glenstall Park could be such a location. He’d pick a place close enough to these cottages to be convenient, but at enough of a distance so it can remain unnoticed by people.”

A buzzer sounded. Paul slid off the counter and walked to the dryer. He tossed Dan’s clothes to him and began to put on his own. “So we only have a few hundred thousand acres to comb.”

Dan finished dressing and pointed outside. “I’ll grab our sneakers.” He stepped out the door and picked up their shoes. Donna appeared from around the corner.

“Well, all warm and dry?” she asked as she came up to Dan.

“Yeah...yeah. Thanks for letting us use the dryer to get our stuff...ah, dry,” Dan stammered. Something caught his attention behind Donna.

Ridgway was heading toward the office.

Dropping the shoes, Dan grabbed Donna and bending her sideways, like he'd seen in the movies, gave her a big kiss, holding her between himself and Ridgway. After a moment of surprise, Donna wrapped her arms around Dan's back.

After Ridgway disappeared to the other side of the building, Dan pulled Donna back to a standing position. She stepped back, smoothing her hair.

"My!" she gasped. "I thought Paul said you were shy with girls."

"I am, but that was an emergency." Dan spun Donna around by her shoulders. "Follow that man who just walked by. See what he's doing. Hurry!"

"But—"

"It's important!" Dan shooed her with his hands. "Please! Go! Go!"

Donna shrugged. "All right."

As she turned the corner, Dan grabbed the shoes and rushed into the laundry. "Ridgway! He's gone into the office. Donna's following him."

Dan tossed the sneakers on the floor. There was a moment's confusion as the twins sorted out which shoe belonged to who. After putting them on, they opened the door a crack. Donna was just coming back.

"Well?" Dan asked.

"He's checking out and—" Donna started.

"Checking out!" the brothers cried out at once. Paul pushed by and jogged toward the parking lot.

"Yes. His stay was over. I told you the resort is booked—" Donna started.

"Thanks for everything Donna you've been a great help but sorry I gotta go I'll talk to you later bye." Dan rushed after Paul.

"Dan! Look out for the—" Donna called after him.

Dan looked behind him and waved. "Thanks! Later!" He faced forward just in time to collide with a tree. He spun off it and caught up with Paul, crouched by the corner of a cottage.

"Back, back!" Paul pushed Dan against the wall. He pointed. "He climbed into that green coupe. It looks a Hudson...perhaps a '34 or a '35."

The car backed out of its parking space and started for the highway.

"A license? Can you make out the number?" Dan whispered.

"Wait...wait until it goes by that Studebaker..." Paul answered. He shook his head. "No dice. The plate is covered with mud."

"Covered with mud! In the middle of summer?" Dan stood away from the cottage. "Let's follow him!"

"Stop!" Dan yanked him back. "Somebody else has the same idea. Look."

A black delivery van pulled out of its spot and trailed after the Hudson. Two men rode in the cab.

Paul gripped Dan's shoulder. "That's the one from the other day! And it was the one that followed me into town. Remember I told you about it?"

"Yes. Let's join the parade." Dan ran toward the jeep, his brother behind.

They piled in, Dan at the wheel. He backed out of their space and drove toward the exit. A sedan towing a travel trailer coming the other way reached there first. It crawled down the single-lane road toward the highway and stopped, its left turn signal blinking.

Dan pounded the steering wheel in frustration. "It'll take them all day to make a left!"

While it didn't take that long, many agonizing minutes dragged by before the car hauling the trailer finally lumbered onto the asphalt. Dan pulled up to the stop sign, and the brothers scanned the roadway on either side of them. Neither the coupe nor van were in sight. The twins groaned in unison.

"Damn!" Dan growled. "Well, that's that. Let's go home and phone Archer again. And we should keep the well business to ourselves. We don't want to be left open to a trespassing charge."

They drove back, each twin's head swiveling as they vainly tried to spot Ridgway's car or the black van. After parking in their driveway, they walked in the back door. Paul headed for the living room. "I'll try to call Archer."

Dan continued toward his bedroom. "Thanks. I have to get ready for work. At least I won't have to take a shower. I'm still soggy."

After he finished changing, Dan returned to the living room. Paul was speaking on the phone.

"Yes, that's right, Mr. Archer. A green Hudson coupe. A black delivery van, a panel one, maybe a Dodge, followed it." Paul listened. "About an hour ago. Sorry, we didn't get license numbers on either or which direction they took. A slow car blocked us at the parking lot exit." He waved his brother over. "Did you want to talk to Dan? He's here. Okay, hold on a second." Paul held out the receiver and Dan took it.

"Hello, Mr. Archer," Dan said.

"Well, Dan, you're doing an excellent job upgrading your badge from junior G-Man status," Archer's voice crackled over the wire. "Paul said you fellows spotted Ridgway out at the lake. He was staying at the cottages there under an assumed name—"

"Ward Wayigredd," Dan put in. "Two 'd's at the end."

Archer chuckled. "Got it. Two 'd's'. Did you catch a glimpse of the drivers of the van?"

"No, but I'd say there were two." Dan looked at his brother. "Paul, two guys in the van?"

Paul nodded.

"Yeah, two in the cab. One was large and...wait a minute," Dan said. "It might have been the same guy."

"What same guy?"

"A couple of days ago, a stranger stopped me after work to ask for a light," Dan recalled. "I didn't have one, so he went on his way. He limped."

"What did he look like?" Archer's question was sharp.

"He was a big bruiser—not fat, just big—with close-cropped red hair," Dan said. "His voice was raspy, and he had some type of accent."

"A foreign one?"

Dan tried to remember. "No. No, it didn't seem like one. He talked more like somebody from a city, like, I don't know, New

York or Chicago. You know, he sounded like a movie gangster, a 'dem' and 'dose' kind of thing."

"Any marks or scars?"

Dan thought for a second. "Yeah. A scar on his right cheek."

"I don't like the feel of this," Archer said, with a hint of dread. "It's possible there are other people after Ridgway's money. The people in the van could be some of them." Dan motioned for Paul to join him by the phone and held the receiver so they could both listen in. "Have you heard of the Dalton brothers?"

"Didn't they ride with Jesse James?" Dan asked.

"Not these two. They wouldn't know one end of a horse from the other," Archer remarked dryly. "These two are Gimpy and Wilbur Dalton."

"Gimpy?" Dan smiled at the name.

"Gimpy is the big one. Walks with a limp. His real name is Thaddeus."

"I can see why he goes by Gimpy," Dan said.

Archer chuckled. "The Daltons were also part of Rizzo's gang, a couple of enforcers...muscle. After the massacre, they struck out on their own. They've done time frequently for racketeering, armed robbery, and various things. I don't know if they and Ridgway overlapped on their respective prison terms. I'll have to check that angle out."

"So if all these jokers met in jail, the Daltons could have found out about Ridgway's stash," Dan said.

"That's right," Archer responded. "If they can take the cash from Ridgway after he recovers it, he won't be able to take legal action against them. What could he do? He can't report it to the police since it's stolen money in the first place. I'm positive the Daltons think that would be a brilliant plan. An easy pile of money for them." He paused for a second. "Do you believe the Daltons think you have ties with Ridgway?"

"I'm not sure how they could figure that out." Dan and Paul glanced at each other. "If they were in the van that passed us when we gave Ridgway a lift, they saw him in our jeep. Gimpy asking me for a match may just be a coincidence."

"Why?" Paul asked.

"I hope they have not marked you down as working with Ridgway—and I hope they do not in the future," Archer warned. "If they come to believe that you are in any way connected to him, it could be dangerous for you. Don't fool with them. I want you to promise to contact the police if they come anywhere near you, okay?"

"We promise," Dan said. "But there's no need to worry. I don't think they could connect us to Ridgway. It must have been clear that we just gave a ride to a hitchhiker."

"Besides, last we saw of the Daltons, they were trailing Ridgway. The whole bunch are miles out of town by now, most likely," Paul said.

"Keep your distance as a precaution if they come back. Don't tangle with them," Archer cautioned.

"We won't," Dan said. Paul nudged him and rubbed his fingertips of his right hand together. "Ah, Mr. Archer, I hate to ask this, but about the—"

"The reward?" Archer finished.

"Well, yes, about the reward...I'm a little embarrassed..." Dan's voice trailed off.

"Don't be," Archer replied, "but I have to recover the money first. If I do, I'll give this information you two have provided me to Worldwide, along with any other tips I obtain. They make the final decision about who gets the payout."

"Oh, okay." Dan looked at Paul and shrugged.

"I'll assign men to cover the highways out of Farmingford," Archer said. "Can I call you back if I have any more questions?"

"Of course," Paul said.

"Thanks for the call," Archer said. "Excellent work, boys. Good bye."

"Bye," the twins chorused back.

Dan hung up the phone. "Well, I guess it's back to mowing lawns for you, and slinging sundaes for me."

"Should that story we're going to tell our children include how we messed up?" Paul asked with a grin.

"Of course not! Instead, we'll tell them we bravely battled Ridgway and both Daltons, and would have won if they hadn't pulled submachine guns on us!" Disappointment tinged their laughter. Dan slapped his brother on the back. "Off I go to toil over a hot lunch counter!" He stopped and turned back. "Oh, be sure to take down that sign outside."

"What sign?"

Dan flashed a rueful smile. "The one that reads 'Case and Case–Tracer of Lost Funds'."

Chapter Ten

Dan's shoulders slumped as he made his way to the jeep. He had wanted his brother and him to surprise their mother with that large reward check, but that seemed to be pretty unlikely now. He lowered himself into the driver's seat, like a balloon losing its helium.

As he drove towards Allen Drug Store, his thoughts about Ridgway and the hidden loot kept pestering him. He wanted to figure out the correlation between Wolf Lodge and this obscure man, even though he would never encounter the gangster accountant again. When he cruised past the ornate Victorian mansion that housed the Farmingford Historical Society, an impulse seized him. He checked at his watch and saw that he had enough time to visit, and so he turned into the parking lot.

The air inside the museum hit Dan with the odor of old books and lemon wood polish when he walked through the leaded glass front door, the coolness of the interior a welcome break from the heat outside. The entry hall was decorated in classic 1890s style, a grandfather clock sonorously ticking off the seconds as it had done for decades.

To his right, an arch opened into a parlor with high ceilings and old-fashioned furniture. Portraits of stern-faced men with beards stared down from the walls, while the specters of dowagers in stiff dresses hovered around the corners, each unsmiling visage labeled and cataloged. A modest collection of antiques and historical memorabilia sat in displays on tables or stood on shelves lining the walls. An opulent chandelier hung from the ceiling, every crystal droplet still intact. A few shafts of sunlight slanted through the north-facing windows, making dust motes sparkle in the air like tiny fireflies.

Dan turned left into the sitting room, now serving as a small gift shop, and he stepped up to the counter. Mrs. Campbell, one of the gaggle of ladies who ran the Society, was fussing with some items in a display. A nest of thin silver bracelets clinked together as she arranged them in the case. Her head was bent at a sharp angle and she swayed as if she were hatching a brood of chicks. She was a slight woman, flighty; Dan always pictured her as a bird flitting from branch to branch. She glanced up and beamed at him.

"Oh, Dan, just the person I wanted to see!" She smiled mischievously as she stood upright and waved toward an empty spot on the wall. "Do you see what's missing?"

Dan looked at where she showed and broke into a grin. "My painting sold!" *At least one good thing happened today*, he thought. Although kissing Donna was high on the list as well.

"Someone purchased it earlier in the day." Mrs. Campbell clapped her hands together and continued excitedly, "He—the customer—was quite enthusiastic about it, said it was very dynamic! He spent a long time here, asking question after question."

"I've finished another painting...another landscape," Dan said. "After I frame it, I'll bring it in. It will just fill the space."

"Oh, that's wonderful!" Mrs. Campbell trilled. "Oh, do let me pay you while you're still here."

"I'll always take the money!" Dan grinned.

Mrs. Campbell walked to the cash register and opened it, the jingling of the bell sounding crass in the refined quiet of the museum. She counted some bills on the counter. "There you go, minus our commission as usual."

Dan signed the receipt and scooped up the money. "Thank you, Mrs. Campbell. A pleasure doing business with you!"

Mrs. Campbell clapped her hands as she laughed. "And you too!"

Dan slipped the money into his wallet. He tried to sound casual. "Oh, by the way, Mrs. Campbell, what do you know about Wolf Lodge?"

"Why, quite a bit." Mrs. Campbell assumed an upright posture. She cleared her throat daintily, folded her hands in front of her and spoke like a tour guide. "The Wolf family were early settlers of this area, with Alfonso Wolf arriving in 1793. They owned substantial tracts of land in this area and grew their wealth through farming and logging. Jeremiah Wolf constructing the lodge in 1896, using timber from the property and rock from a nearby quarry. It's still there, only it's nothing more than a pit in the ground now, but it exists."

"Jeremiah was the last of the Wolf family," Mrs. Campbell continued. "Unhappily, his brother Edward lost his life in the infamous sinking of the Titanic in 1912, and Jeremiah passed away in his sleep in 1922. Since they had no offspring or relatives to assume their legacy, so the estate was all sold off piece by piece at an auction. One parcel was bought by a Mister—"

"What happened to the lodge?" Dan prompted, trying to hurry the docent along.

"Oh, the lodge! That was ever so exciting!" Mrs. Campbell exclaimed, clapping her hands. "There was a lot of interest in the property at the auction. Records from the time say the bidding was fast and furious! The price climbed higher and higher and higher until there was a single bidder remaining, Mr. Samuel Ashton. Everybody was positive he won it. But it was not to be!"

She paused for dramatic effect. "The auctioneer was about to bring the hammer down when a voice from the back of the room spoke up, offering a huge sum. Thousands of dollars more than what Mr. Ashton had bid. He couldn't match it and the mysterious man from the back of the room took it."

"Who was the winner?"

"It turns out the bidder wasn't the actual buyer. He actually represented someone from Chicago. The man, who was apparently quite unremarkable looking, blended into the crowd during the auction. Nobody paid him any heed. He was silent until he called out his own bid. He refused to identify the purchaser, but it came out after he filed the deed. It's a public record, of course, and with the notorious blabbermouth Mrs. Daniels at the recorder's office, the truth came out quickly." Mrs. Campbell's eyes glittered with excitement as she leaned toward Dan and asked, "Can you guess whose name was on it?"

Dan shook his head.

"It was none other than Lorenzo Rizzo!" Mrs. Campbell nodded her head for emphasis.

Dan's scalp tightened. "Lorenzo Rizzo!"

"You've heard of him?"

"I've...I've heard the name."

"Then you may know his reputation: bootlegger, racketeer, mob boss. He was quite infamous in the annals of Chicago crime," Mrs. Campbell declared.

"Has anyone ever been able to identify who the mysterious representative was?" Dan asked, although he had a strong hunch of his identity.

"Not by name, no," Mrs. Campbell admitted. "They say Rizzo employed him as an accountant or bookkeeper or in some such role."

Eddie Ridgway! Dan couldn't believe it. It made sense. He had discovered a missing piece of the puzzle, the connection between Ridgway, Rizzo, and Wolf Lodge. It was difficult to keep the excitement out of his voice. "Did Rizzo spend time out there?"

"That all depends on how you define it," Mrs. Campbell dropped to a secretive tone, as if she was sharing an especially juicy bit of town gossip with Dan. "Rizzo ran an illicit gambling joint out of the lodge, but one reserved only for a very particular group of high-roller VIPs. By invitation only. It was all kept very exclusive. He also provided other, um, additional 'services', shall we say, to his clients when they laid down their money. Plus, there were whispers that he used the property as a place to store his smuggled bootleg liquor."

"What about the police? Didn't they do anything about Rizzo?"

Mrs. Campbell gestured in dismissal with one hand. "Rizzo was untouchable! Not only did he have his fingers in all the pies, he had in his entire hand! He bought and paid for all the law enforcers and politicians in the area. He ran all his operations with no opposition until..." She mimed firing a machine gun. "Rat-ta-ta-tat!" After making a show of her pantomime, she returned some out-of-place strands of her hair back to their ordered positions and appeared pleased with her performance. "Rival mobsters rubbed out Rizzo out in 19—"

"1929," Dan finished automatically.

"Why, yes! You know of it!"

"I got it in history class," Dan lied. "What happened to the lodge after that?"

Mrs. Campbell let out a sigh. "Not much. Actually, nothing was ever done with Rizzo's estate. It never was resolved, other than, of course, providing steady jobs for an army of lawyers. Then the stock market crashed in October 1929, followed by the Great Depression, then Germany's Führer came into the picture and everybody forgot about the property until the state seized it for delinquent taxes."

The grandfather clock in the hall struck four.

"I'm late for work!" Dan hurried for the door. He turned to wave. "Thanks for the history lesson, Mrs. Campbell!"

Dan sprinted to his jeep and watched the speedometer climb as he raced to the drugstore. When he arrived, he flung open the door with so much force that its little brass bell shook on its bracket as though it was going to rocket across the room. Mr. Allen paused in stocking shelves and pinned Dan with a stern look from behind a pair of round, smudged glasses.

"Sorry I'm late," Dan called out as he jogged toward the soda fountain. "I know, I know, kids nowadays. Don't tell me."

Dan apologized to Ted as he took his place in back of the counter. He tried to concentrate on his job, but his thoughts kept diverting to Ridgway, Rizzo and Wolf Lodge. He kept coming back to the same conclusion he and Paul arrived at that afternoon: Ridgway must have hidden his loot somewhere around the lodge. But where?

Each new idea sparked excitement, yet a part of him reasoned against it. Ridgway did not know of the disposal of Rizzo's estate or how long it could take to settle or what the future of the lodge and its land could be. Dan ran through different scenarios with the lodge as the starting point of a treasure trail or of loot hidden somewhere on the land.

Stop thinking about that, Dan scolded himself. *At least you sold a painting. Ridgway got away...again. It's a done deal. But where could that money be?*

The sound of a coffee mug hitting the cold tile floor, followed by the rapid clatter of shattering pieces, startled Dan out of his daydream. He glanced up, hoping Mr. Allen hadn't seen or heard him. He crouched down, gathering jagged shards of the evidence in his hands and quickly dumped them into the trash.

"You young people nowadays," Dan imitated his boss' voice to himself, "you don't know the value of things. Do you think money grows on trees?"

No, Dan thought, *but it could be buried under them.*

Dan didn't have a moment to spare for any more deliberations. The first showing of the movie at Farmingford Bijou a few doors down the street had just let out, and it seemed the entire audience descended on the lunch counter at the same time. Dan was rushed off his feet, serving coffee, scooping ice cream, distributing slices of pie and making sandwiches. So busy was he that when he finally looked up, he realized it was closing time.

Dan wiped down the counter and put away the last of the dishes from the evening rush. He dumped his tips out of the cup he stashed below the cash register, running his fingers through the coins and bills with a satisfied sigh. Having worked hard all night paid off, but nothing compared to getting that big reward...

He stepped outside the drugstore and took a breath. The night was a deep blue, the stars overhead burned fiercely. A sliver of orange moon hung low in the sky, its light brushing a few strands of silver clouds. He drove home slower than usual, simply enjoying the night, putting all thoughts of hidden money, treasure trails, and gangsters out of his mind.

He pulled into the driveway, the tires crunching the gravel beneath them. After he set the parking brake, he squinted at the workshop. He thought he saw a glimmer of illumination from the window, but decided it must have been a reflection of the jeep's headlights. Unlocking the back door, he stepped into the darkened kitchen. As he shut the door behind him, the eerie tones of the spooky "Lights Out" radio program echoed from the living room.

"Dan?" His brother called.

"No, it's Edward Ridgway," Dan answered. "Where's my money?"

"You've come to the wrong house, pal!" Paul laughed. "How was work tonight?"

"Busy, but it paid off in good tips. Oh, and I also sold a painting." Dan removed the apron and tossed it on the breakfast nook table. He got a glass of water from the sink.

"Good for you!"

"Not only that, I found out some—" Dan glanced out the window over the sink, the glass almost to his mouth. A small circle of light, like from a flashlight, glinted in the workshop's window. He put down the tumbler. "—information on the town's history."

That can't be a reflection, he decided. He poked his head into the living room and lowered his voice. He motioned to his brother, sprawled on the sofa. "Paul! Get in here! Quick! No, leave the radio on!"

Paul got up. Dan held an index finger to his lips, and returned to the kitchen window. When Paul joined him, he pointed to the workshop. The glass was dark again.

"What?" Paul peered into the night. "What's up?"

"I think we have a visitor in our workshop," Dan whispered.

"We do? Where?"

The ball of light reappeared and danced around inside like a will-o'-the-wisp. "There!" Dan pointed.

"We'll see about that." Paul turned toward the door, and Dan grabbed his arm, shaking his head.

"Wait." Dan rushed into the living room and switched off the radio and the lamp, plunging the house into blackness. He went back to Paul. "Maybe whoever it is will think we've gone to bed," he whispered.

Paul nodded, then jerked his head to the backdoor. He crept over, Dan behind. Paul had just grasped the knob when Dan noticed something through the glass pane, which made up the top part of the door.

"Wait!" Dan hissed. "More company! Over there!"

The twins peered through the window and spotted a figure creeping from the side of their house, along the fence that bordered the backyard. It stopped for a moment, then dissolved in the shadows that lingered under a sprawling oak tree.

Paul's fingertips hesitated on the doorknob, then opened the backdoor a sliver. The brothers slipped through the narrow opening, Dan's hand holding his brother's shoulder, squeezing, unnecessarily sucking in his stomach, hoping the screen door wouldn't produce its characteristic rusty squeak. The door closed behind them with only a soft click. Dan held his breath even after they had made it through. They flattened themselves against the kitchen's back wall, swallowed by the total blackness under the service porch roof.

The door to the workshop cracked open. A tall, slender silhouette of a man, only slightly darker than the night, stood in the doorway, then stepped outside like a ghost. A light breeze rustled the leaves.

Paul took a step forward, but Dan put out one arm to stop him, pointing to the other side of the yard. The unknown person lurched from his hiding place in the shadows and shot toward the figure who had just left the workshop. In an instant, their dark forms became entwined in front of the garage door. For a moment, Dan couldn't tell what was going on.

The two figures entangled in a wild embrace, their grunts and shuffling feet echoing through the empty alleyway. The intruder from beneath the tree tried to grab hold onto his opponent's clothing, but kept losing his grip. Meanwhile, the man from the workshop attempted to pry off the other's clinging hands, pummeling them with his fists. As they struggled, they crashed into the garage door with a loud thud, sending it rattling. Without warning, the tall and thin figure broke away and tore down the drive leading to the street, followed by the second person.

Dan and Paul shot out of the porch, ready to take down their unwanted guests. But when they reached the bottom step and headed for the driveway, a fierce grip clamped down on the back of their necks, lifting them off their feet. They were shaken like rag dolls before being tossed aside.

Paul crashed into a garbage can, while Dan stumbled over the coils of the garden hose which wrapped around his feet like a boa constrictor. Struggling to get to his feet, Dan's foot snagged on the hose again, pitching him toward the ground. He attempted to keep his balance by grabbing Paul, only succeeding in taking them both down. Untangling themselves and staggering back upright, they charged down the driveway in pursuit. The sound of an engine roaring to life ripped through the air, followed by screeching tires as a car sped away.

The brothers sprinted over the sidewalk, not stopping until they reached the center of the pavement. To their left, there was an empty street, with a car's taillights giving them one last mocking farewell before it took the corner.

"We should be in the circus. Our act would be two clown cops trying to catch some crooks," Dan muttered in disgust as he brushed his clothes off.

Paul opened his mouth to speak, but stopped as their shadows suddenly loomed on the asphalt in front of them. A loud engine roared from behind. The twins whipped around to meet a pair of blindingly bright headlights speeding towards them.

Without thinking, Dan grabbed Paul's arm, and yanked him toward the sidewalk, the two sprawling onto the grass with a grunt. The sound of the vehicle whooshed past. With a quick glance up, Dan glimpsed what almost hit them: a black delivery van.

Chapter Eleven

"Did you see who any of them were?" Dan got to his feet, then helped his brother up.

"No," Paul growled as he brushed himself off, "but I'll lay you even odds the car was a green Hudson coupe."

"Followed by our friendly neighborhood delivery van we saw earlier," Dan added. "Driven by the Daltons, I'm sure. Aimed, more like it."

"The person coming out of the garage was tall and slender. It must have been Ridgway," Paul said. "If so, it means the whole happy crew didn't beat it out-of-town today, like we thought. Why are they hanging around? What did they want at our house?"

Dan gestured toward the garage. "Only one way to find out, my dear brother, only one way to find out."

The twins rushed back to the workshop, hoping to uncover what their mysterious visitor had stolen and what damage was done. Dan tried the door. It was unlocked. He reached in and switched on the light, a single bulb in the ceiling.

Paul examined the doorknob. "It doesn't seem forced. It's an old lock, so he must have used a skeleton key."

Dan grunted a response and stepped inside. It surprised him nothing was out of place. Everything was in its usual spot, untouched and orderly, as though nothing had happened at all.

"Ridgway must be the neatest burglar of all time." Paul planted his fists on his hips as he looked around.

Dan scanned the room once again. Something caught his eye.

"Not quite." Dan checked the small table. "Somebody has rummaged through my sketchbooks. I stack them with the spines facing out, away from the wall. Look. One of them is reversed, with the binding the opposite way."

Paul leaned in to see. "Are they all there?"

Dan counted the stack. "Yes." Noticing something on the floor, he got down on his knees to check beneath the desk. He retrieved a piece of paper with a mountain sketched on it. "It came out of one of my books. Whenever I draw something I like on a single sheet, I put it in a sketchbook so I don't lose it."

"Do you know which book that sketch came from?" Paul peered over Dan's shoulder.

"I'm not sure." Dan waved a hand over the books. "It could have been any of them. I don't date them or mark them at all, except maybe the location." He glanced around the workshop to make sure he didn't miss anything else.

"Let's check through those books," Paul said. "If we can figure out which one held the sketch, it may give us an idea what he was looking for."

Dan nodded, and the two pored over the books. After a short time, one page drew Dan's attention.

"See this?" Dan handed an open book to Paul. He ran his finger down the ragged edge where a page had once been. "Something had been torn out."

Paul checked. "It sure has. Do you remember what was on it? What it was a picture of?"

"I'm stumped." Dan shrugged as he brushed his eyes over the drawings as he flipped through a couple more pages. "They're all of Wolf Lodge. They're the ones I did them for the Historical Society a few years—" He dropped the sketchbook onto the table with a thud, "That's it! That's it!"

"What's it?"

"Wait a minute, wait a minute." Dan lifted his palm to stop the conversation. He thought for a moment. "Okay, I learned something at the museum today. I didn't get a chance to tell you before tonight's show started, but listen to this little news scoop." He shared the information Mrs. Campbell told him about Rizzo and Wolf Lodge.

Paul let out a whistle. "So it's logical Ridgway would be familiar with the lodge."

"He has to be," Dan agreed. "At least enough to be the mysterious bidder at the auction. When Rizzo ran the place as a gambling den, Ridgway may have taken trips from Chicago here as part of his work. You know, to collect the winnings or check the books or something."

"So years later, his embezzling scheme falls apart, most likely when the brewery demanded an audit," Paul picked up. "He need-ed somewhere to hide the money he skimmed fast, and remembered the lodge."

"He must have known that Rizzo's estate was still stuck in the courts and up in the air, so the lodge was still available. He scoops up the cash and hauls it down here to squirrel it away until everything blows over. Or until he could move it to a different place, but he went to jail instead," Dan added. "Mrs. Campbell also told me Rizzo's mob used the lodge for smuggling bootleg booze. Ridgway probably knew of those hiding places."

"Those bootleggers were crafty in stashing their stuff," Paul said. "Perhaps there's a secret cellar..."

Dan shook his head. "No, I still don't think he hid it in the building. There were too many unknowns about the final disposal of the property. Not to mention his own future."

"There are caves in the park," Paul said. "One of them could have been used to hide bootleg liquor, and now Ridgway concealed his money in it."

"That makes sense, but which cave, though? Where?" Dan drummed his fingers on the table in thought.

"Did you see some kind of map when you did your work for the Historical Society?" Paul asked. "I mean, was there one in the building? A mural or something?"

"No. I think I would remember that," Dan said.

"Then where does the lodge fit in?" Paul asked. "If he didn't hide the money in it, that is?"

"I was thinking about that at work. I can't shake the idea of some type of map must be involved. Ridgway's a city slicker. He's not going to become Davy Crockett and find his way through the wilderness. Even experienced hikers get off track every once in a while. He would need precise directions. It's possible that the lodge is his starting point. The first step in a series of instructions." Dan imitated a pirate. "'Har...first take ye ten paces west from the gnarled oak tree.' You know, that kind of thing. Somewhere around that place there is a secret path which leads to his cash."

"Let's just say it's in a cave." Paul sat on the stool. "It would be hard for Ridgway to rediscover it after some time. Even if it's a few minutes after leaving, it may be tough to find the entrance again. Especially if it is hidden away in a remote corner filled with trees and brush and such. The landscape barely changes over time, but it changes. Trees fall over. There could be a landslide. Maybe it's not a paper map Ridgway used. Again, that could risk being lost, destroyed or stolen. He would need to mark the actual path to his cache. Something physical."

"And it couldn't be too obvious to tourists visiting the park, yet sturdy enough to last for years and against the weather," Dan said. "So he might be using subtle signs like notches on trunks, rocks placed at regular intervals, and so on. Ridgway could find and follow it because he'd know what to look for and where to start. How does that sound?"

"I'll buy that, but there's something else," Paul added. "Some of the deeper caverns have been sealed off for safety reasons. Wouldn't that cause problems for Ridgway?"

"Well, I doubt he would mind that. It would serve as a bank vault," Dan said. "I'm sure one little old padlock wouldn't stop him from getting in."

Paul nodded.

Dan went on. "The sign or pointer for the first step was located in Wolf Lodge, somewhere, but the fire damaged or destroyed it. Something I sketched on that page he tore out provided that missing clue."

"What a minute." Paul hopped off the stool. "How did Ridgway know to come here? How did he get our address?"

Dan considered that. "Remember when we picked him up at the gas station?"

"Yes, but we didn't give him our names."

"That's right, but he thumbed through my sketchbook."

Paul nodded. "He said how much he liked your work."

"He also saw the drawing of the lodge, how it looks today," Dan said. "He asked me about it. Then I mentioned I had done some art for the Historical Society."

"And?"

Dan leaned toward his brother. "And I'll bet if I describe Ridgway to Mrs. Campbell, she'll identify him as the purchaser of my painting. I sign my art, so all he had to do was read my signature. Next step: look us up in the phone book to get the address. We're the only 'Case' family in town."

"I'll go for that. Now where do the Daltons fit in? Ridgway must get they're on his tail," Paul said. "Certainly he does after tonight."

"Like Archer told us, Ridgway may know them from the Rizzo gang days or jail," Dan said. "Maybe Ridgway thinks the Daltons are not the brightest things on two feet, so he can outsmart them." He let out a sigh. "I wish I could remember what I drew on that piece of paper."

"Yeah." Paul ran his fingers through his hair. "That would make everything—"

"The snapshots!" Dan said.

"What?"

Dan was already heading for the door. "Snapshots, snapshots! I took photographs *and* made sketches of Wolf Lodge! The pictures were for reference later if I wanted to do a painting. I keep them in my desk."

Dan raced to his room, with Paul only a few steps behind. He yanked open the bottom drawer and rummaged through a pile of photograph envelopes until he found the packet he was looking for. He opened it, pulled out the photos, and handed half of them to Paul. Their fingers moved quickly through the stack, flipping each one over with a soft rustle of paper filling the room.

"Wait, what about this one?" Paul passed a photo to Dan. It was a close-up of the Wolf Lodge fireplace mantle. "Isn't there something in the wood?"

"Hmm, this may be it." Dan studied the picture intently. "I'm sure I sketched it and took a photograph also, because it was so strange, or maybe it had some historical importance." He pointed to the series of symbols etched across the mantle. "They don't appear like they're well crafted but done by someone with a penknife, almost like graffiti." He tapped the photograph against his thumb while he thought. "We found a pencil on the hearth in the living room. I remember seeing Ridgway carrying a creel up there, and before I was knocked out, I saw it stuffed with sheets of paper beside the mantle."

"So Ridgway could have taken the paper and pencil to the lodge to copy down these symbols," Paul said. "Or do what I've seen you do sometimes…take a rubbing. Those designs may be his first step."

"You could be on to something."

Paul examined the picture. "They remind me of, I don't know, symbols used by Indians. I wonder what they mean."

"I know! I bought a postcard when Dad took us on that camping trip before he went into the army." Dan headed for his desk again. "It was about Indian symbols."

"Do you hang on to everything?"

Dan pulled himself up to his full height and spoke in a cultured voice. "Frederic Remington owned a vast collection of Indian artifacts he used for his art. Remember, sir, I too am an artist. I save items which may provide a spark of inspiration for my next masterpiece."

Paul rolled his eyes. "Oh, brother."

"Yes, I am." Dan rummaged through a drawer, extracting the postcard. "Here it is. 'Indian Symbols and their Meanings.'" He sat back down on the bed. "Now, what's on the mantle?"

"On the left, there is a circle…a kind of wagon wheel," Paul said.

Dan scanned the postcard. "That represents 'hogan', a permanent home."

"Just under that is a wavy line, and above it a jagged line." Paul thought for a moment. "Easy. Water and mountains, with the house between. That would fit the lodge. The lake is in front, and the mountains are behind."

"That's sounds about right," Dan said. "What's next?"

"Then there is an arrow, pointing right."

"Arrow, pointing right," Dan mumbled to himself as he checked the postcard. "Here it is: 'protection.' Then what?"

Dan squinted at the photo. "It seems like hoof prints, a lot of them...let's say, ten sets."

"Are they from a deer?"

Paul nodded. "Sure."

"The postcard says 'plenty game'," Dan said after checking the card. He looked at his brother, puzzled. "Huh? The lodge needed protection from plenty game?"

"Perhaps they were being menaced by a particularly vicious herd of deer," Paul answered.

Dan gave his twin a shove. "Give me a break. Anything else?"

"Something that looks like a plus or a cross, but not filled in. Then another arrow pointing up," Paul said.

"The plus sign means 'paths crossing'." Dan scoured the postcard again. "Nothing about an arrow pointing up."

The two were silent for a moment. Finally, Dan spoke. "I'm lost. I can't make heads or tails from it. Any ideas?"

Paul shook his head. "Not a single one. We could be on the wrong track. It could be they don't have a meaning." He shrugged. "Some prankster or drunk carved the signs into the mantle as a joke."

"Or we're over thinking the whole thing," Dan suggested. "The arrow may not stand for 'protection', but it only means 'go that way—to the right of the lodge.'"

"Okay, then what about the hoof prints?" Paul tapped the pho-to. "Walk until you run into a herd of deer?"

Dan thought, then an idea came to him. "What is a hoof?"

"It's the foot of ungulate mammals."

Dan arched his eyebrows. "Wow. Go to the head of the class. A foot is also twelve inches."

Paul frowned. "So, wait, you're saying that each hoof represents a foot in distance? Ten hoof prints equals ten feet?"

"Forget a foot. That would put the trail about ten feet from the lodge. Probably too close." Dan thought for a minute. "A hoof has two sections, so that's two feet per hoof." He shook his head in disbelief. "Bah. Even then, we're still only twenty feet away."

"Or it could be ten feet per hoof, or one hundred feet per hoof. Without some kind of key, there's no way of knowing," Paul was quiet for a second. "It could refer to time, not distance. Something like 'Walk for ten minutes.'"

"Time is not as precise a measurement as distance. People move at different speeds. The hoofs still could represent a particular unit of measurement. We just need to figure out what it is," Dan said. "That whole park is crisscrossed with trails, fire, and old logging roads. So you leave from the right side of the lodge and walk for the specified distance, as shown by the deer tracks, to a specific intersection of paths marked by the cross. You ignore any others between. You'd enter the cross from the left side. The up arrow could mean that the next sign is on the trail to the left, or one the one in front of you."

Paul nodded. "I'll buy that."

Dan scooped up the photos and put them back in the envelope. "You know what? I'm in the mood to get up early and get in some fishing out at the lake."

"That's funny. So am I." His brother stood and grinned. "I'll pack a measuring tape in the tackle box. Start at five a.m.?"

Dan got up and flashed Paul a grin. "Five a.m."

***

The brothers reached Wolf Lodge at six in the morning. The rising sun painted the trees a pale, light pink, like a blush spreading across the leaves. A cool breeze swept over the land, ruffling their hair and skin. They inhaled deeply, enjoying the freshness of the morning. The air was clean, with only the smoky aroma of a fire coming in from the campground.

"The right side of the lodge." Dan placed one palm on the building's stone wall. He grabbed one end of the measuring tape Paul held up.

Paul backed away, counting off each foot as the tape unfurled until he reached ten feet. He clicked the lid shut and set the case down onto the earth. He observed his surroundings. "No hint of a path here."

"Okay, let's walk that distance at our normal pace, and count about how many steps it takes to cover the distance," Dan said. "Then we can estimate how far we traveled and not take measurements all the time."

After checking the number of footsteps they took, Paul bowed to Dan. "After you."

"No, no. I insist," Dan replied, bowing lower, "after you."

The two walked away from the building, the crunch of their footsteps on the dry, gravel ground mixed in with the singing birds and the occasional caw of a crow. They left the clearing surrounding the lodge and entered the woods. The trees shaded them from the morning sunlight as they advanced farther in.

They trekked through the woods, dodging low-hanging branches, wading through tall grass and pushing past bushes, counting their footsteps, stopping every ten feet, their eyes scanning their surroundings for any sign that marking the intersection with Ridgway's trail, without finding anything. Keeping in the same direction, they stepped out of the forest, picking up a winding path that curved in from their right and ran straight ahead.

When they reached about eighty feet from the lodge, they noticed another path crossing the one they were on. Dan and Paul exchanged excited glances and searched around the edges where the paths crossed, hoping to locate some kind of marker to show Ridgway's route. After several minutes, they found nothing.

"Not a blessed thing." Dan took a swat at a bush, his voice hollow with disappointment. "Do you want to go on?"

Paul blew out his breath and shook his head. "No, why bother. There's nothing here. We could keep on this path for a hundred feet, a hundred miles, and not find a thing. At least Ken will get a new name for us out of this: The Failure Twins."

"Well, let's go," Dan said. As he turned, something caught his attention on a nearby tree. He stepped forward and peered closer at the bark of the trunk, his eyes widening when he spotted something metal embedded in it. "Paul, here."

He pointed to what appeared to be an old iron spike with a number engraved on its surface–"7".

Just as Dan bent over, a gunshot rang out from somewhere near. The brothers froze and looked up. A second later, the bullet struck the tree with a thud, narrowly missing Paul's shoulder.

Chapter Twelve

"Down!" The twins hissed the word and pulled each other to the ground.

"Stupid hunter!" Paul snarled. "This isn't deer season. I've got a good mind to—"

Dan hurriedly placed his hand over his brother's mouth, stopping any sound from escaping. He leaned in close, his whisper barely audible. "We don't know who it is. It might not be a hunter."

Paul's forehead creased with concern as he grabbed Dan's wrist and pulled his hand away. His voice was low. "Are you saying it could be Ridgway?"

Dan nodded, then added, "Or the Daltons."

Paul squinted, shading his eyes with one hand, his eyes darting around the area. "So there could be one or two shooters running around," he muttered.

Dan gripped Paul's arm. "Listen!" He sucked in his breath as a branch snapped in the distance, followed by a silence so intense he could hear the blood pounding in his ears.

The slow, quiet rustling of leaves began again, the sounds growing nearer, with every step filling Dan with ice-cold fear. Then, just as suddenly as it started, the sound stopped and an ominous silence once again filled the air. The forest seemed to be waiting for the curtain to rise on the next act.

Dan tensed, his head turning left and right as he strained his ears. He picked up the crunching of leaves, the rustling of branches, and the occasional snap of a twig—someone was stealthily making their way through the dense forest toward them. Dan's hand fell on a rock. He grasped it, knowing it wouldn't be much help against a gun, but its heft was reassuring. Out of the corner of his eye, he saw his brother tense like a coiled spring, his hands doubled into fists. The leaves crackled and twigs broke as something got closer with each step. Dan didn't dare to breathe.

A huge buck crashed out of the bushes, its velvet antlers glittering in the dappled sunlight. The brothers rose, glanced at each other, and broke into relieved laughter.

Another shot rang out, the bullet splitting the bark of the tree just behind them. The boys dove to the ground, flattening themselves against the forest floor, and the deer plowed through the woods. Everything went quiet again. Dan and Paul remained still, not daring to move.

"It was a hunter! The idiot!" Paul snarled under his breath.

"Then he must have the world's worst aim. Neither one of those shots came anywhere near that deer," Dan said. "We're the targets, buddy."

The two exchanged glances.

"We need to make it to the lodge," Paul whispered. "We'll be safe there, or we can make a break for the campground."

"At least one of us needs to get back," Dan stressed. "We have to split up."

His brother didn't answer, but forced a ghost of a smile before slipping away through the thick brush. Dan waited motionless for a fraction of a second before moving off in the opposite direction, crouching down and slipping through the undergrowth with his heart pounding. He moved quickly and quietly, not daring to glance behind himself.

A sharp crack shattered the air and Dan dove for cover behind a fallen log, his breathing as loud as a hurricane. The shot ricocheted off a tree to his left. Adrenaline surged through Dan's veins as he realized the bullet must have been aimed at his brother, not him. He forced himself to remain silent, biting down hard on his lower lip to keep from instinctively shouting out Paul's name and revealing his location.

Perspiration trickled down Dan's forehead as he scoured the area, his muscles so tense he believed his bones would snap like matchsticks at any minute. An unseen enemy was hunting for him, filling him with dread and uncertainty. Death could be behind any tree. He balled his hands into fists, his fingernails digging into his palms, wondering if this was how his father felt in combat before he was...

Dan shook his head, ordering himself to put that idea out of his mind. Then, in the distance, movement rattled the brush. He peered over the top of the log, but couldn't tell who was making the noise. He realized he could use the noise—whoever made it—as a cover for his own movements. It provided an opportunity to get out of there. He hurried away, stopping when the other noise did. After a second, he continued.

He navigated between the trees and bushes on silent feet, careful not to break any twigs or knock any rocks. His breath caught in his throat. There was more rustling. He held his position, not daring to move until he heard movements growing softer in the distance, with luck the sound of the hunter moving away. After what seemed an eternity, Dan exhaled, cautiously straightening his crouched form.

He pushed off with a burst of energy fueled by fear, sprinting as fast as he could. He leapt logs and dodged trees, branches scratching his cheeks and whipping his hair. When he spotted the clearing ahead, he felt a rush of relief and changed direction towards the lodge visible in the distance. He took off in its direction, feeling mixed waves of relief and anxiety. A voice hailed him.

"Dan!"

Paul emerged from the shadows of the lodge's well house. Dan jogged over to him, waving and grinning with relief.

"Are you all right?" Dan asked as he caught his breath.

"Yeah, except for a couple of scratches from branches," Paul answered. "You?"

Dan nodded. "Same here. Did you see who it was?"

Paul shook his head. "No, but I'm certain there was only one."

"I guess that leaves out the Dalton brothers, unless they only have one gun between them and they share it, which doesn't seem likely." Dan leaned against the wall and blew out his breath. "So

the man behind the gun must have been Ridgway." He thought
for a second. "He steals the sketch of the fireplace mantle, giving
him the first set of directions to his hiding place. Not thinking we
had another copy, he didn't expect us to pop up here. Then we go
and surprise him. He takes potshots to scare us away from the area,
because we're on the right trail." He glanced at his brother. "No
pun intended."

"Good." Paul pointed toward the trees. "Do you want to go back
and pick up the tracks?"

Dan shook his head. "Not with Harold the Happy Hunter
prowling around out there. I don't want to end up stuffed and
mounted over his fireplace."

"Maybe we should check the parking lot again, see if we missed
spotting his car this morning," Paul suggested.

"There weren't a lot of cars when we drove in," Dan said. "We
should have seen it."

"Yeah. It's clear he beat us here, but parked somewhere else."
Paul slouched against the wall. "Since Rizzo used this lodge and the
woods around it to smuggle and store his bootleg booze, it would
be logical that the gang probably avoided the major highways
when hauling the stuff here. Most likely they'd choose the logging roads, backwoods trails and such. Ridgway must know about
those routes. He could drive out here without going through the
park entrance."

Dan gestured at the sprawling expanse of trees. "There are miles
and miles of roads out there. Some are blocked by fallen trees or
landslides, or abandoned over the years, but we can't trace every

single one. What do we do now?"

"We should report an unsafe hunter to the ranger station, at least," Paul said. "Even give them Ridgway's description so they can be on the lookout for him."

"That sounds like a plan," Dan said. "We need to put a call into Archer, too, and bring him up to date. I doubt he could get out here any time soon. And we still didn't have any definite sighting of Ridgway as the shooter."

"I vote him the ace number one suspect, at any rate." Paul checked the area. "It appears to be empty." The sound of children's laughter filled the morning air. "Great. Some tourists are on their way up here. Ridgway won't risk doing anything with onlookers. I hope."

The two left the shade of the outbuilding. They headed past the lodge, toward the drive leading to the parking lot. There were a few moments of quiet as they walked along.

"Paul?"

"Yeah?"

Dan looked at his brother. "Were you scared? Out there in the forest?"

Paul met Dan's gaze. "I nearly peed myself."

"Me too."

The twins exchanged grins, then burst out laughing. They hurried to the ranger station, speaking with urgency as they explained their encounter with whom they called an unsafe hunter, providing details of Ridgway's appearance. The ranger promised to keep an eye out for him. After reporting the incident, they walked back toward their jeep, making a detour through the entire parking lot first.

"Not a green Hudson in sight," Paul noted.

"I didn't expect to find it," Dan said. "Did you?"

Paul sighed. "I suppose not."

"We're great at smacking into dead ends." Paul punched one fist into his open palm. "Pow! We must be setting a world's record."

Paul gave a small shrug. "I don't know. We'll just have to hope the insurance company finds our evidence convincing enough to give us the reward."

"Bah," Dan grumbled.

"You don't work today, do you?" Paul asked as they stopped by their jeep.

"No, I'm off. Why?"

"Because we're going on that double date tonight," Paul nonchalantly announced.

"What! After what we've just been through?"

"We've told the rangers about Ridgway prancing around the woods taking wild shots at people. They have jurisdiction out here. We're done," Dan said. "There's nothing else we can do, is there?"

"No," Dan acknowledged after a moment.

"Betty and Donna want to see the Fred MacMurray picture, *The Egg and I*. It's playing at the Majestic in Belmont," Paul said. "So..."

"When did you dream up this little plot, Mussolini?" Dan sputtered.

"The day we set up your meeting with Donna," Paul responded.

"You're despicable!" Dan raked his fingers through his hair. "And you didn't tell me? Huh? Why?"

"Because, my dear brother, I knew you'd be worrying about it for days, so that's why." Paul smiled and jerked his thumb toward the woods. "You looked more scared about this date than when we were being used for target practice."

"I am!" Dan retorted.

Paul laughed. "You've been on dates before."

"But not with a girl like Donna!"

Paul draped his arm over Dan's shoulder. "Don't worry about tonight, Dan. You don't need to put on an act or pretend to be someone you're not. Donna likes you, the real you, my friendly, funny, artistic identical twin brother with those dreamy soft brown eyes and, in particular, those floppy ears." Dan gave him a dirty look. Paul chuckled and patted him on the back. "Just relax and be yourself."

"All right. I guess I'm stuck." Dan smiled and took a deep breath. "It's still early. Let's do some fishing. So the morning isn't a total loss."

"I'll buy that," Dan said, "but at a place where there's plenty of people."

***

Betty drove her family's convertible with the top down, its stowed canvas roof rustling in the wind, the moonlight and stars glittering against the night sky. Sitting beside her, Paul sang along to the music from the crackling radio, while Dan and Donna laughed in the back seat. They joined in the singing, with Dan imitating the voice of Pa Kettle, a character from the movie they'd seen that night.

The car roared through the night, headlights cutting through the darkness. Forests, pale and silent, flew by in a blur, broken only by the occasional yellow warmth spilling from a distant farmhouse window. About halfway between Belmont and Farmingford, the red neon glow of a sign reading "Midway Motor Motel" came into clearer focus, the 'd' in the word flickering like a dying firefly. Next to the motel was a small, all-night diner shaped like a railroad dining car with two glowing windows, and to the left of it was a sprawling farm supply dealer with a combine perched atop the roof.

Dan's eyes automatically darted to the right as they drove past the line of businesses. The song caught in his throat when he spotted a green Hudson parked in front of one of the small motel rooms. He almost reached out to tap Paul on the shoulder and point it out, but he realized he'd have to explain why it was so important. He wasn't sure he was ready for Betty and Donna to know about Ridgway.

His mind snapped back to the conversation in the car and joined in, only to be disappointed to see they had arrived at Betty's house much sooner than he expected. As though planned, Dan and Paul jumped out of the car in unison, running to open the doors for the girls and bowing deeply.

Paul checked his watch. "Check the time! We still have five minutes before curfew."

The couples strolled up the walkway. Dan and Donna stopped at the stoop, while Paul and Betty went up to the porch.

"I enjoyed going to the movies with you, Dan," Donna said as she took his hand.

"Yeah, so did I. It...it was fun." Although Dan's nerves had calmed somewhat during the evening, they still fluttered in his stomach like lost butterflies.

"You remember what happened outside the laundry room?" Donna asked.

"Well, yeah, sure. We saw the guy." Dan hoped he didn't blush again. "He's my dad's old Army buddy friend..."

"That's who you said he was," she reminded him. "But I'm thinking about when you saw him."

"When I...oh, that."

"Are you still shy?" Donna winked.

Dan shuffled his feet and gave an awkward laugh that almost sounded like a donkey. "Yeah."

"Don't be," Donna hinted.

Their eyes connected and their faces inched closer together until their lips softly pressed against each other. When they broke away, their fingers remained intertwined and Dan smiled, not caring whether he looked goofy. From the corner of his eye, he spotted Paul and Betty locked in an embrace.

"Hey, hey, you two, break up that clinch," Dan pointed to the crack between the curtains covering the living room window. "The referee is on the job."

The girls said their goodbyes to Dan and Paul before heading inside, leaving the brothers to walk to their jeep. Dan took his place at the wheel.

"Well, how was that, sport?" Paul gave Dan a light punch on the arm.

"I will admit I had fun, my dear brother." Dan flashed a grin. "Thanks for setting it up. And making me go."

"Anytime, handsome," Paul said. "You didn't act nervous at all. Other than spilling the popcorn over everybody."

"Hey, it was dark in that theater!" Dan protested.

"Go ahead. You stick with that story. I'll never tell." Paul stretched and yawned. "Anyway, it will be sweet dreams tonight."

Dan started the jeep and zipped down the street. He downshifted as he approached the intersection with Linden, his arm leaning on the edge of the door. When he reached the corner, he swung the vehicle to the right.

Paul gave Dan a puzzled look and gestured in the opposite direction. "Our house is over there," he said, showing the left side. "What made you go this way? Did that kiss from Donna cause your brain to turn into chicken mash?"

"Our house may be over there, but the Midway Motel is out here," Dan pointed out.

"Why? What's at the Midway Motel?" Dan asked.

"A green Hudson coupe," Dan said.

Paul grabbed the steering wheel and yanked it hard to the right, pulling the jeep over to the curb.

"What's the big idea?" Dan shouted.

"We are not going to the Midway Motel," Paul declared.

"Maybe *we* aren't, but *I* am." Dan pried Paul's fingers off the wheel. "If you don't want to, fine. Get out. Walk home."

Paul took a deep breath and released it. "Dan, it's time to face facts."

Dan turned to his brother. "Facts? What facts?"

"We're not the Hardy Boys," Paul said in exasperation.

"What do you mean by that?" Dan demanded.

"What do you mean, what do I mean? I'll tell you. It's simple. We're not detectives," Paul said. "We should leave ferreting out the bad guys to the professionals, like Archer."

"The professional isn't doing a whole heck of a lot better than we are," Dan argued. "Why should we stop?"

"You said it yourself this morning," Paul said. "We've run into nothing but brick walls. We haven't made any actual progress in this business since we started."

"No progress!" Dan jabbed a finger at Paul. "Oh, yeah? What about getting dunked in the well? What about the theft of my sketch? What about becoming shooting gallery clay pigeons this morning? All that happened to us because we were making no progress? Somebody must think we are!"

"That still doesn't mean we are on the right track," Paul shot back.

"What other track could it be?"

"Somebody doesn't want us nosing around, that's for sure," Paul said. "And frankly, that's good enough for me. I'd like to graduate from high school in one piece."

"I never figured you for a quitter," Dan spat out.

"That's not true and you know it," Paul fired back. "There's a difference between giving up and accepting reality. It's time to say it out loud: Ridgway's won."

"He hasn't yet." Dan crossed his arms.

"He has! Don't you understand?" Paul yelled. "Ridgway has outmaneuvered us throughout this entire business. He's beaten us every step of the way. All we can do is wait to see what Worldwide says about what we've told Archer."

"And what about Mom?" Dan challenged.

"What about her?"

"We both know just how hard it has been ever since Dad was killed," Dan said in a quiet yet intense tone. "Sure, you and I have our jobs to kick in some cash and help take care of the three of us, but Mom has had to carry most of the load by herself. Look at all the work she's done, is doing, to hold this family together. Is that really fair? Don't you think she deserves this reward money to make her life a little easier? Shouldn't we try our hardest to earn it? To give it to her? To help her? It is the least we can do for her, isn't it?"

Paul leaned forward, his body tensing as he stared at the floor mats. "That's hitting below the belt, Dan," he said through a clenched jaw.

"Yes, it is," Dan's voice was calm. He looked at Paul. "But I know my brother. I've seen him in the ring, taking blows that he shouldn't have taken, but refusing to give up even when it was clear that he was outmatched. I admire his courage and how he slugs it out to the final bell."

Paul was quiet for a moment and gave a rueful smile. "You landed some pretty hefty blows yourself." He gestured over the hood of the jeep. "All right. Let's get to the Midway Motel."

Chapter Thirteen

The twins drove out to the motel, parking next to some trees on the opposite side of the highway, out of the neon sign's glow. Dan hopped out. He lifted the jeep's hood and propped it open.

"In case we're asked by somebody, the engine overheated." Dan brushed his hands off. "We're waiting for it to cool down."

Paul nodded as he came up to his brother. The two gazed at the motel.

The motel's design was an attempt to evoke Colonial style—so much so that you'd expect a sign out front that read "Ye Olde Office." Red brick and white trim made up the building, with a long porch connecting all the twenty rooms of the one-story complex, built in the shape of an "L", with the office separate in front. Wooden columns rested atop stone blocks which held up the outdoor hallway. Flower pots hung from hooks between each post, filled with vines that sprouted fragrant night-blooming flowers. The parking slots in front were full of cars.

Dan pointed to the corner where the building's two wings met. "See there? The green car?"

"Yes," Paul said. "But is it the same one? I mean, there's more than one green Hudson in the world. That one could be owned by a traveling salesman."

"It's his, I tell you."

"So what do we do?" Paul shrugged.

"Well, one—" Dan grabbed Paul's arm. "Look!"

Ridgway pulled open the door of his room. He stepped out and stood in the pool of yellow light that spilled from the porch lamp. After locking the door, he moved across the asphalt with slow, deliberate steps towards the diner next door.

"Like he does not have a care in the world," Dan muttered.

Paul nudged his twin. "While he's having dinner, we can get his car's license number, at least."

"Excellent thinking, my dear brother!" Dan said. "It's good to know you haven't taken too many blows to the head."

Paul responded with a punch to Dan's arm.

"Ouch. Your right is also excellent." Dan rubbed the spot and glanced down both sides of the two-lane rural highway. He took a step to cross it, only to draw back and grab Paul, pulling him behind the jeep.

"What was all that about?" Paul complained.

"It was about a black panel van," Dan answered.

"Where? Which way was it heading?" Paul poked his head above the fender.

"South."

"I don't see it."

Dan peeked over the jeep. The quarter moon cast a dim light on the road. It was empty. The night was clear and free from engine noise, though the steady hum of crickets filled the air.

"It's gone now. Let's get that license number." Dan stood up and closed the jeep's hood. A moment later, they were both walking swiftly across the pavement.

"We're going for a cup of coffee while we wait for a tow," Paul said in a low voice.

"Understood," Dan replied.

They cut through the motel's parking lot, strolling toward the illuminated window of the diner. As they passed the rear bumper of the Hudson coupe, Dan dropped to a knee and made as if he was tying his shoe. As he did, he reached over and wiped the mud from the rear license plate.

"Got it," Paul murmured after staring at the numbers.

Dan rose to his feet, and the two moved together in the direction of the diner's friendly aroma of grilled burgers and onions. "Boy, I'd love to see inside Ridgway's room."

"I believe that is called 'burglary'," Paul said.

"No, I was thinking more along the lines of a Peeping Tom."

"Oh, well, that makes all the difference."

Dan glanced over his shoulder and saw light escaping from the room through the slats of the closed blinds. "Sealed tight," he said to himself. A thought occurred to him. "There are windows, aren't there—on the far side?"

"I'd guess so. For the bathrooms, most likely," Paul said.

They made it to the end of the motel building. Another two hundred feet of open space lay before reaching the diner.

"Anybody nearby?" Dan said.

Paul looked around. "Nope."

"Come on," Dan said. "At least it's worth it to see if we can find out anything."

They entered the empty, narrow strip of land running between the brick motel and a six-foot concrete block wall that marked the outdoor yard for the farm supply store. It was a dead end, blocked by a storage shed.

The overgrown weeds were dry and tall. They whispered and crackled as the brothers walked through them, mixed in with the sound of crickets and radios playing from the rooms.

Dan stopped and pointed to the end of the wing. "That must be Ridgway's room—right there."

Dan and Paul ducked down, staying close to the ground as they inched their way down the motel. The light spilling from some of its windows cast a soft glow on the weeds. They reached the spot Dan had showed earlier—next to the last of the illuminated windows.

Dan slipped up along the wall, peered through the insect-splattered screen of the window. His suspicions were confirmed—it was the bathroom, but its door was wide open, allowing a direct view into Ridgway's room. He took a deep breath and stepped forward, his shoes crunching on the gravel beneath his feet. Paul joined him, standing shoulder to shoulder.

The bed was still made, the bedspread smooth and unmarred. No suitcase or other personal items were visible. The blinds hung listlessly against the windows, and nothing moved aside from the occasional breeze through the room.

"He must be the perfect guest," Paul observed. "He touches nothing in the room."

Dan whirled around and put his hand over Paul's mouth to keep him quiet. Out of the vacant strip of land that stretched behind them came a clattering sound like an old tin can, followed by a muffled curse that sounded similar to an aged hinge.

As a truck rumbled by on the highway, its noise settling, an eerie stillness cloaked the area. The only one that remained were two voices speaking in hushed tones. One voice was raspy. Dan recognized it.

"The Daltons!" Dan's eyes searched for a place for the brothers to hide. The weeds, although tall, weren't big enough to conceal them. Cautiously, he pulled Paul towards the wall and pointed up. Paul nodded, jumped, and climbed. Straddling the top, he held out one hand and helped Dan. They dropped to the other side and leaned against the concrete blocks.

For a few minutes, they couldn't hear anything except their own breathing, then footsteps rustled through the undergrowth. The rhythm of them seemed off; one firm step followed by a soft shuffle as if two feet were not in sync, or one foot was dragging along the dirt behind the other.

Dan put his lips next to Paul's ear. "Gimpy." Paul nodded.

The footsteps halted. The brothers stood on their tiptoes to peek over the concrete block, across the open strip of land toward the motel. They saw the silhouette of a large man flattened against the brick wall. With caution, Gimpy leaned in, his head turning to the right and to the left, looking through the glass into Ridgway's room. He was searching the interior, finding it empty—just as the twins had done before.

Gimpy abruptly stopped trying to stay secret. He pulled on the screen and pushed up the window, allowing the brothers a quick view of the stocky man as he wedged himself through the opening. Dan tapped Paul's arm, pointing towards another smaller figure smoking a cigarette at the far end of the building.

"That must be Wilbur down there," Dan whispered. The two slipped back down the wall. He sighed. "I guess we're stuck here until they leave."

A low, throaty growl came through the night.

"Ha, ha, ha. Hilarious," Dan hissed. "Now shut up."

Paul leaned toward Dan. "That wasn't me."

Dan's eyes darted around the yard, trying to pierce the thick darkness that shrouded the farm equipment, crates, and bales of hay. Something rustled in the night and Dan's body stiffened. An animal slowly separated from the shadows.

The guard dog's lips curled back in a snarl, revealing razor-sharp fangs. The beast lowered its head menacingly and unleashed a deep growl that echoed through the night air. It fixed its eyes on the two with an icy glint of the hunter, promising violence should they dare to move.

The brothers remained still. The dog took a couple of steps closer as it continued to snarl and bark.

"Over the wall?" Paul said out of the corner of his mouth.

Dan shook his head. "That would deliver us smack in the arms of the Daltons."

"Well, we can't stay here."

"No need to state the obvious." Dan glanced to his right. "See those hay bales? Let's get on top, out of Fido's reach."

"Do you think we can make it there in time?"

"Only one way to find out," Dan said grimly.

The brothers scrambled to their feet and ran for the hay; the dog barking and chasing them. They hopped onto the first bale and quickly made their way to the second, their churning sneakers sending bits of straw fluttering to the ground. The dog leapt at them, coming within inches of taking a chunk out of Paul's ankle as he climbed up to the higher bale. As they reached the summit, Dan glanced back and saw that the dog had stopped short of jumping up after them with a frustrated bark that echoed through the night air. They had evaded Fido—for now.

Their breath came in short gasps as they pressed their bodies against each other on top of the hay bales, trying to make themselves as small as possible.

Dan nudged Paul. "The window."

Gimpy emerged from Ridgway's room. He stood in the middle of the weeds, looking around carefully. It appeared their luck had held out; either he didn't see them or he wasn't sure where exactly to look. They stayed deathly still until his footsteps, crunching on dirt, faded into silence as he walked away.

"I wonder if he found anything," Dan said.

"Who cares? What do we do about Fido down there?" Paul asked.

Dan shrugged. "I don't know. Got any dog biscuits on you?"

"Gosh darn, I'm fresh out," Paul said. He paused before he went on. "How about you run one way to distract him while I go over the wall?"

"Me? Why don't *you* distract him, and *I* go over the wall?"

"Because artists are probably tastier."

"Oh, yeah? You've got bigger muscles, so you would be a veritable Fido feast."

"Well, we'll have to come up with something soon. Somebody's going to call the sheriff, with all the noise that dog's making. It would be awkward to explain to a deputy how we ended up here."

Dan checked the area behind him. "How about this? We crawl to the end of this stack of hay. We jump down on that tractor's seat, then climb those crates over there next to the wall. Then up and over."

Paul looked over the route. He sounded doubtful. "I don't know. One false step, and we become a doggie treat."

"Do you have any other bright ideas?"

Paul took a deep breath, grinned, and slapped Dan on his back. "You know, it's a wonderful idea! It's great! I'm in love with this idea!"

The two crawled along the top of the hay, each bale swaying as they shifted their weight. Fido paced around them at the base of the stack, fur bristling and snarls rumbling from his throat. Finally, Dan reached the last one and plopped himself onto the edge. His heart raced as he stared down at his target below, which seemed to have shrunk to the size of a pea. The dog took up a position between the tractor and stacks of hay, its body tense and alert. He pulled his lips back in a silent growl, revealing sharp white teeth.

Dan sucked in some night air and let it out slowly before launching off the bale. His feet connected with the metal seat with a clang. He tried to keep his footing but was thrown off balance and dropped into a crouch, arms flailing about to steady himself, almost pitching backward.

Throwing his weight forward, Dan lunged and planted his palms against the stack of wooden crates, leaning out as far as he could to increase his reach. The dog ran in circles around the tractor, barking wildly, its teeth snapping.

"Now I know how a treed raccoon feels," Dan muttered to himself. It wasn't a pleasant feeling.

Two-by-fours held apart the boxes by a few inches, leaving a gap between them. Next step: swing over Fido's head and get a toehold on those crates.

Dan shuffled his hands up the side of the crate until they rested on the lid and used that as an anchor to swing across. His toes slid into the gap of the crate below once he was secure. He reached up with one hand, then the other, until he grasped the next crate up and scrambled higher, as if climbing a cliff. He repeated his moves, at last pulling himself on top of the stack.

He sat on the edge, grinned, and gestured his brother over. "Come on in, the water's fine!"

Paul jumped onto the tractor, only to have his right foot slide off. Immediately, the dog charged over, and Paul regained his footing on the seat after a brief struggle.

"Are you okay?" Dan asked.

"Yeah. Fido just got part of my pant leg," Paul answered. "Here I come!"

He leapt to the crates. Dan got down on his stomach and offered a hand to Paul, helping him to reach the top of the stack. They were now higher than the wall. The two eased themselves back down the concrete blocks and touched the ground again.

Dan waved a dismissive hand at the barking dog on the other side. "Aw, shaddup! Ya mudder wears army boots!"

Paul pointed. "Let's get behind those trees where we can't be seen from the motel. Wait until Fido calms down. We don't want to get spotted in the area in case somebody is wondering what all the commotion is about."

The two jogged over to the woods and sat down in back of some bushes. Paul examined the frayed cuff of one of his trouser legs.

"Damn, my best pair of pants." He leaned back against a tree trunk. "What do you think the Daltons wanted in Ridgway's room?"

"It must have been searching for some kind of clue to the location of the loot," Dan said. "I doubt he was after the family silver."

"Like Archer said, Ridgway has done nothing illegal after getting out of prison. Until he picks up that embezzled money," Paul said. "Trying to pin burglary on Gimpy would not only be a waste of time, but could also alert Ridgway that we've found him."

Dan listened. It was quiet. "Fido seems to have retired for the night, dreaming about his missed meal, most likely. Let's head back to the jeep and figure out our next move."

The brothers used the trees for cover as they moved to the deserted highway. They quickly crossed and returned to their jeep. Paul examined the motel on the other side of the road.

"Only a few room lights still on, including Ridgway's," Paul said.

"Maybe he's afraid of the dark," Dan said.

"Or he could be having another piece of pie." Paul looked toward the diner. "There's a moving van parked in front that's blocking the window. I can't see if he's still inside."

"Now that we really have that guy nailed down, I don't want him to slip past us another time," Dan said. "Twice is enough."

"So we need to sit tight and keep him under observation," Paul said.

Dan nodded in agreement. "That's the plan, but maybe one of us should go home and try contacting Archer's office."

Paul checked the luminous dial of his watch. "It's late. Will it be open?"

"I don't think so, but there may be an answering service," Dan said. "It's possible we'll be here all night, so who knows what could take place? No one can remain awake forever. Ridgway has got to go to bed, eventually."

"I'll be on duty first, then. I'll hide behind that." Paul pointed to a billboard advertising train travel that stood nearby. The sign was four feet off the ground with white lattice work filling the gap between the bottom and the dirt. He told Dan the coupe's license number and Dan repeated it back.

"Right, got it. I'll be back in a flash." Dan climbed into the jeep and started it.

"Bring a thermos of coffee. We'll need it." Paul started toward his hiding place.

Dan hunched over and gripped the steering wheel tightly. He pressed his foot down on the pedal until it hit the floor. The engine roared in protest as he hurtled down the empty highway. He threw his head back and laughed in triumph—Ridgway wouldn't be able to escape for a third time. They had him cornered! The detective firm of Case and Case always got their man!

He screeched to a halt in front of the house and leaped out of the driver's seat. Fumbling with the keys in his excitement, he unlocked the door and burst inside, stumbling past furniture and knocking over a vase on the way to the living room. He snatched up the phone with one hand as he clicked on the desk lamp with the other. He dialed the long-distance operator and gave Archer's number. The phone at the other end rang and rang and rang while Dan scribbled down the license plate on a scrap of paper, then tapped the pencil's eraser impatiently against the desktop as he waited.

"Come on, come on." He chanted as if in the stands at a football game. "Answering service, answering service, answering service."

A woman's voice, speaking in precise, rounded tones, came on the line. "I'm sorry, sir, but your party isn't answering."

"Thank you, operator." Dan tossed the pencil back on the desk. "I'll try again later."

Dan headed into the kitchen and started a pot of coffee. After changing into jeans and a dark blue tee-shirt, to help him remain unseen during his stakeout, he hoped, he returned to the stove and poured the steaming liquid into a beat-up thermos. Soon he was back on the road to the Midway Motel.

Dan drove alone down the long stretch of highway. Occasional truck headlights illuminated the darkness, and a few stars sparkled in the night sky along with the crescent moon. He pulled the jeep onto the shoulder of the road and stepped out into the dirt. The diner's window was dark, and the light in Ridgway's room was still one of the last showing.

"What a night owl," he said to himself. He called quietly, "Paul?" After a couple of seconds of silence, he tried again, a little louder. "Paul!" Dan walked through the tall grass toward the billboard. "Did you fall asleep, buddy?"

He pushed his way through the vegetation that grew next to the sign, emerging into the clearing behind it. Empty. Suddenly, a burlap bag was pulled over his head, squeezing around his neck like a noose as powerful hands held it in place, cutting off his airway.

"Not a sound, pal, if you know what's good for you," a raspy voice spoke in Dan's ear.

Chapter Fourteen

Dan held his hands up in surrender.

"Bright boy," Gimpy growled.

"Where's my brother?" Dan demanded.

Gimpy twisted the sack tighter. "No talkin'and get on your knees."

Dan attempted to resist, but Gimpy's strength was too great. He knelt while Gimpy looped a rope tightly around his wrists and bound him securely. Then, a smothering sensation engulfed Dan as a gag shoved the burlap bag into his mouth, filling him with an overwhelming sense of dread. Any cries for help were muffled by a relentless cloth gag, and Dan knew that no one would hear him—apart from Gimpy, that is.

"On your feet." Gimpy yanked Dan up by one arm, almost ripping it out of its socket. He pushed Dan forward. "Walk."

Dan stumbled ahead with each step, nearly tripping over rocks and dips in the terrain. Gimpy laughed at Dan's missteps before shouting, "Stop!" He had barely gone a few feet.

The sound of a handle being turned, followed by the squeal of two doors opening, pierced the air. Gimpy grabbed Dan and, with brute force, forced him down onto the cold metal floor of the delivery van. He crossed Dan's ankles, tied them together and heaved his captive back into the vehicle as if he were a sack of mail. Dan's breathing came in ragged gasps as terror overcame him.

Dan sensed somebody else occupied the cargo area. He tried to call through the gag, "Paul?" He was relieved when a muffled, if not understandable, response came in his brother's voice. That calmed him down a little; at least he and Paul would face what was coming together,

Gimpy took hold of the front of Dan's shirt and yanked him into a sitting position. "I said no noise, includin' chattin'," he roared before striking him with his open palm and shoving him back to the floor again.

A second, higher-pitched voice spoke. "Is everything at the ready? Are the packages secure?"

"Yeah, Wilbur. All set," Gimpy said. "I'll stay in here with 'em and make sure they're all comfortable like while we take them for a little ride."

Gimpy's raucous laughter reverberated around the tight confines of the cargo area as Wilbur produced a polite chuckle. The van jostled as Gimpy climbed in, squeezing his bulk between Dan and Paul with the exhausted groan of somebody who had put in a hard day's work. The slam of the doors echoed, locking shut with a final click. A minute passed, then Dan heard the driver's door open and close again. The engine roared to life, and the van lurched forward, its wheels spinning in gravel and bouncing through the dirt before surging out onto the paved road. Soon, the smell of cigarette smoke filled the air.

Dan wriggled as he tried to become at least a little comfortable, triggering a warning growl from Gimpy. His heart raced at the thought of what he'd gotten himself and Paul into. Archer's warnings echoed in his memory: getting mixed up with the Daltons was a dangerous mistake. He did not know what would happen next or if he'd ever look back on this decision with regret. Or be able to. He wished he hadn't talked Paul into continuing their pursuit, but most of all, he regretted putting his mother through all of this. She already lost her husband; now she might lose her sons too.

As the van rumbled down the highway, Dan's mind raced with possibilities. He tried to remember if he had left any clues to let the police track them down. Was there any way out of this? He forced himself to concentrate, to push the fear to the back of his brain, and resolved to be on the lookout for any chance of escape.

Gimpy lit up another cigarette and blew the smoke into Dan's face. He coughed and wanted to turn his head, but the gag kept him from doing so. Gimpy chuckled at Dan's discomfort.

After a while, the vehicle slowed and made a left off the smooth roadway onto a bumpy dirt road. Dan could feel his stomach lurch as they bounced over the potholes. The van crept along the uneven surface, then made a right turn.

A right after leaving the highway...remember that, Dan thought to himself. *That could be helpful.* He paid attention to the direction of travel, something to do to occupy his brain, to make him believe he was accomplishing something useful...and take his mind off what could be coming. *Another right, a left...the van is going slower, the ride getting rougher...we must be on a poorly maintained dirt road...*

The silence was thick with tension, broken only by the grumble of the van's engine and the occasional curse from Gimpy as the vehicle navigating the rough terrain jostled him.

After what seemed like an eternity, the van came to a stop. The back doors opened and Gimpy slipped out. After he and Wilbur conversed in low tones, Gimpy announced to his captives, "End of the line! Everybody out!" He laughed.

"Escort our guests inside," Wilbur said.

There came a sliding sound as they pulled Paul out of the van. A grunt from Gimpy, as though hoisting something, followed by heavy footsteps fading away. The van's doors slammed shut.

Dan struggled toward them, and put his feet out, trying to feel if there were any interior handles. He only encountered smooth metal. He pushed against the doors, to no avail. They were closed tight. Before he could think of anything else, they screeched open again.

He felt himself being dragged out of the van, his body sliding along the steel floor as he was pulled out. Gimpy threw Dan over his shoulder like a sack of potatoes. Dan squirmed as he tried to see the surroundings through the burlap bag. They appeared to be in a clearing, tightly surrounded by trees and dense underbrush, in front of a small wooden cabin. Gimpy began walking toward the porch, the sound of his footsteps changing from crunching on dirt to a dull thump on wood porch boards as he hauled Dan up the steps.

The two stepped through a door, into a flickering yellow, orange light. Gimpy thrust Dan down on a chair, its legs creaking against the floor. The glint of a switchblade danced in front of the burlap before Gimpy cut and tore away Dan's shirt, securing Dan to the chair with a length of rope looped just below his chest. The gag and bag were removed. Dan spat out some burlap fibers and looked around.

The cabin was tiny and spartan, most likely used by hunters in season. Its bare wood walls had a few fading animal pelts hung as decoration. A bunk bed was partially built into one corner, its sturdy frame holding tight to the wall. Paul stood roped to an upright post at its foot, his shredded shirt at his feet, along with the gag and burlap sack. Dan sat next to a small round table that held a kerosene lamp.

Seated across from him in the only other chair was Wilbur Dalton, his appearance a stark contrast to his brother's. He was smaller and had neater, and most likely expensively, styled hair. His sharply tailored suit was in stark contrast to Gimpy's shapeless one. Wilbur busied himself cleaning his nails with a switchblade, unconcerned with everybody else present—only the little finger of his hand holding the knife extended gracefully. Gimpy closed the cabin door and leaned against it, the wood creaking at his weight.

"Are you all right?" Dan asked Paul.

Paul nodded. "You?"

"Okay."

An ominous silence draped the room as everyone waited for Wilbur to finish the last of his fingernails. He inspected the result with satisfaction, folded the blade and placed his coat pocket.

"What is all this about?" Dan demanded.

"We wish to have a friendly conversation, that is all," Wilbur flashed a smile, anchored by a gold tooth.

Dan sputtered in anger and struggled with his bonds. "Friendly! You call this how to have a friendly conversation?"

"I have a proclivity toward efficiency," Wilbur said. "I prefer having everything properly configured if the discussion becomes, shall we say, discourteous?"

Gimpy reached behind Wilbur's chair, into a black canvas bag. He extracted a blowtorch, placing it on the table with a metallic thud, its brass glowing dully in the lantern light. A chill ran through Dan.

Wilbur tented his fingers. "By preparing my partners for such unpleasantness early in the conversation, it functions as a harbinger, a foretaste to them, of what may occur at a time in the future. It also tends to eliminate the tedious 'you will not make us talk' soliloquies, because they come to the realization quite soon we will force them to tell us all that they know." He chuckled. "Actually, they frequently beg to tell us more than we wish to know to make us stop." He waved one hand at the blowtorch. "This serves as a reminder that it behooves them to be cooperative."

"'Behooves'," Gimpy chortled. "That's a funny one, Wilbur. You love them fancy words." He pointed at Wilbur and declared to Dan and Paul with obvious pride, "He does the crossword puzzle in the paper every day, including that big one on Sunday. And no cheatin' either. He fills out the whole thing, all the boxes, short ones, long ones, all of 'em."

"How remarkable," Dan remarked dryly.

"Yeah, ain't it." Gimpy beamed at his brother in admiration.

Wilbur gazed at Dan and Paul. "Before we commence, I must comment that the resemblance to Slick is remarkable." He leaned toward Gimpy. "Do you not agree their appearance is similar to him when he was their age?"

"You bet. They're dead ringers," Gimpy responded. "It's like seeing Slick double after I drank too much of Rizzo's bad hooch."

"Slick? Who are you talking about?" Dan asked.

"You do not know?" Wilbur asked in surprise. "Why, we are speaking about your father, of course."

Dan and Paul looked at each other, puzzled.

Wilbur turned to Gimpy. "My, my, examine their expressions! It is as if they were unaware of their father's background."

"Our Dad's name was Tony, not Slick," Paul said.

"Tony, Anthony, Slick, it is of no material difference." Wilbur shrugged. "Names were not of particular importance in Rizzo's organization."

"Yeah, especially when dealing with the coppers," Gimpy put in.

"True," Wilbur nodded. "Not knowing an associate's actual name was quite advantageous in encounters with the local legal authorities."

It took a moment for Dan to find his voice as the implication of what Wilbur said sunk in. "Wait, wait a minute. Are you telling us that our dad was a member of Lorenzo Rizzo's gang? No, no, you got that wrong. Our father worked at the bank in town, as a teller."

Wilbur and Gimpy laughed knowingly. "It figures Slick would end up where all the lettuce was!" Gimpy hooted.

"Slick joined the syndicate when he was approximately 15," Wilbur said to Dan after they had calmed down. "He initially ran numbers and was very adept at his work. Very organized. He was rapidly promoted due to his competence and skills."

Gimpy chuckled. "And man, that guy could talk his way out of any trouble."

"Hence the reason he became christened with the moniker 'Slick'," Wilbur continued. "Slick impressed Rizzo, so much so the boss mentored him. Treated him like his own flesh and blood...almost like a son. He was ready to promote your father higher within the organization prior to the occurrence of that unfortunate June incident, which halted everything."

Dan sat in stunned silence, torn between the news his father had been part of Rizzo's gang and not wanting to accept such a possibility. He felt numb, as if he had lost something crucial to him and that he had been betrayed in some way.

"That's not true!" Paul strained against the ropes. "Dad would never do something like that! He'd never be involved with people like you!"

"People like us? People like us! Hey, I don't like the sound of that punk! Now get this and get it straight." Gimpy stalked over to Paul and poked his finger in Paul's chest, emphasizing each word. "Your old man was nothin' but a cheap, no good, two-bit hood."

"Like you?" Paul spat back.

Gimpy roared in rage and backhanded Paul across the face so

hard his glasses flew off.

"Leave him alone!" Dan yelled.

"Gimpy, please. Not yet," Wilbur sighed.

Gimpy turned on his heel and went back to Wilbur. "Sorry."

Paul's head dropped to his chest, his voice a quiet moan. "He wasn't a cheap hood, he wasn't...not Dad..."

Dan glanced at his brother with concern before turning his attention to Wilbur. "What do you want with us? You didn't bring us out here to tell us our family history."

"You are correct in your assumption...I am sorry, which one are you again?" Wilbur said.

"Dan."

"Ah, Dan, and that sibling over there must be Paul. I confuse you two. Your appearance is so similar," Wilbur said. "Nevertheless, I am desirous of information concerning your activities assisting Mr. Ridgway."

"Assisting Ridgway? What do you mean? We're not working with Ridgway," Dan said. "Where did you come up with that bright idea?"

"Allow me to remind you of a few facts." Wilbur held up his index finger. "One, Ridgway exited the bus at the gas station, met you and your brother there, and you two drove him into town."

"You've got to get your eyes checked, pal," Dan returned.

"My visual acuity is perfectly adequate," Wilbur said with a touch of irritation. "You are not going to attempt to convince us we did not see Ridgway riding in your vehicle when we passed you on the highway, are you?"

"No, of course not," Dan said. "But Ridgway didn't set up a meeting with us—"

"Do not prevaricate," Wilbur snapped.

Gimpy chuckled. "'Prevaricate'. That's a good one." He repeated the word under his breath.

"Shut up." Dan glared at Gimpy, then spoke to Wilbur, "I'm not...prevaricating. We offered him a ride. He didn't ask for one."

"So I am supposed to accept that Rizzo's accountant randomly happened to have a rendezvous with the sons of Rizzo's protégé at an out-of-the-way highway gasoline station where they were randomly filling up at the same time and he randomly asked them for a lift into town and they just as randomly agreed?"

"It was a coincidence!" Dan cried out. "We didn't know—"

"Do not treat me as a fool," Wilbur's voice dripped with contempt.

"I'm not! Coincidences happen!"

"Similar to the meeting between you, your brother and Ridgway, held in the public library? Yes, we are aware of it. Was that a mere coincidence as well?" Wilbur's face was hard.

"What are you talking about? We didn't have any meeting with him, at the library or anyplace else," Dan said.

"We followed Ridgway to the library. After a half-hour, we saw him leave, climb into his automobile and drive away," Wilbur stated in a level, controlled tone. "Mere minutes later, you two exited the building. What are we to make of that? That we witnessed nothing more than a fortuitous occurrence of all three of you in the same building at the same time?"

"Paul and I were looking up newspaper articles about Ridgway's past," Dan said in desperation. "Somebody was listening to us, but we didn't know who exactly. It must have been him."

Wilbur clucked his tongue in disapproval. "And why did we discover you at the motel?" Wilbur held up a hand to stop Dan from answering. "Do not tell me. Another coincidence? Of course it was. Or perhaps you just happened to be visiting a sick old maiden aunt staying there, completely unaware that Ridgway was also lodging at that establishment? Or could it be possible you were there for another meeting, a planning session, perhaps?"

"I swear we're not working with Ridgway! We just gave him a ride into town, that's all!" Dan said, his tone urgent.

Wilbur pushed on. "It could be it was not meant to be to plan your next move, but a negotiation caucus about this." He reached into his coat pocket and slapped a piece of paper on the table.

Dan looked at it. "My sketch!"

"The one stolen from your house, which Gimpy in turn re-moved from Ridgway's room tonight. Therefore, allow me to submit for your approval an alternate hypothesis: you went to the motel to steal this item back. It must, therefore, represent something of significant importance." Wilbur tapped the drawing. "You will inform me of everything you know about Ridgway and the location of his money, or things will become very unpleasant. For both of you."

"We don't know where the money is!" Dan said frantically.

"I am losing my patience with your fabrications and evasions, boys." Wilbur gave a weary sigh, shaking his head. "However, so be it. Gimpy, let us demonstrate to these two what the consequences are of crossing the wrong people."

Gimpy pumped the handle of the blowtorch several times, then fumbled through his coat pockets, finally producing a book of matches. He placed one between his fingers, yanked it away from its cardboard backing, and, with a quick flick of his wrist, lit it. Holding it in front of the blowtorch's nozzle, a large, orange flame erupted. "It will take a few seconds before it's ready to use," he said to Dan apologetically. "It has to warm up."

Dan watched Gimpy's every action in a silent terror, his lungs squeezed until he couldn't breathe, his eyes hypnotized by the dancing flames. He fought to free himself from the trance, at last breaking away and looking at Wilbur.

Gimpy held the blowtorch steady and adjusted a small, red knob at the end of the nozzle. The flame sputtered and shifted from an orange glow to a bright blue, sharp jet that crackled and hissed.

"Begin with that one." Wilbur pointed at Paul, then turned to Dan and smiled. "Do not worry. You will also have a turn. I must be fair."

"Don't you dare touch him! Keep that away from him!" Dan fought against his restraints.

Holding the blowtorch in front of him, Gimpy walked toward Paul. Paul sucked in his breath and his eyes widened as Gimpy approached. He turned the blowtorch towards Paul, sizing him up. "I think I'll start at your belly, and work my way up, and save that good-lookin' mug of yours until the end. Your eyes will be the last to go."

"Go ahead," Paul dared in a firm voice. "I can take it. Do your worst."

"Oh, I will, pal. I will," Gimpy replied.

The blue flame danced and flickered in front of Paul's face. He flinched at the heat, took a deep breath, and braced himself. He looked straight ahead, face set, his jaw clenched.

"Your brother better start talkin', or things are goin' to get really hot for you," Gimpy said to Paul. He stopped, then he laughed. "Hey...hey, Wilbur, I made a joke! Did you catch it? I says 'really hot for you' with me holdin' a blowtorch! Get it? 'Hot'? That's a good one, ain't it, Wilbur?"

"Most humorous. You should be on the radio." Wilbur sat back in the chair, folding his hands across his stomach, like an audience member waiting for a concert to start.

"I keep telling you! We don't know anything! Ask Ridgway! Why don't you use your torch on him?" Dan yelled.

"It is a fatal mistake to underestimate Mr. Edward Ridgway, as many have discovered to their lasting dismay. He did not become Rizzo's right-hand man because of his charming personality. He is ruthless, has a will of iron, and would force us to kill him before he talked. You two, on the other hand..." Wilbur didn't finish the sentence, and waved one hand toward his brother. "You may proceed."

Chapter Fifteen

Gimpy swept the blowtorch's angry flame six inches from Paul's stomach. Paul sucked in his breath and a grimace of pain passed over his face.

"Stop! I told you! We're not working with Ridgway!" Dan shouted.

"Then explicate those extraordinary coincidences," Wilbur said calmly.

"We've been following him, but not working with him." Dan's eyes flicked between the blowtorch and his brother. "We wanted to find where he hid the cash."

Wilbur flashed a triumphant smile and motioned to Gimpy. Gimpy pulled the blowtorch away from Paul. "Ah, at last I believe you." He spoke to Gimpy. "It appears we have rivals. These two coveted all of Ridgway's money for themselves. They truly are Slick's offspring."

"No, we didn't want all of it," Dan shot back. "We were only after the reward money."

Wilbur cocked one eyebrow. "You are apprising me of the fact you did not desire all three hundred thousand dollars?"

Dan almost fired back *we're not like you*, but thought better of it. "We figured if we told the private detective tailing Ridgway where the cash was, we'd earn the reward the insurance company offered. We wanted it to help our mother."

"Ah, ain't that cute?" Gimpy sneered. "They just wanted to help their poor, sick old mudder. Say Wilbur, do you think it's the same dame Slick was supposed to have run off with?"

Wilbur held up one hand to stop his brother. "Please, Gimpy, please. You are speaking of these young men's maternal parent. Do exhibit some deference to the role. Do not refer to her as a 'dame'." He turned to Dan. "And how fruitful has your exploration been to find Ridgway's money?"

"Pretty much a failure, I'm afraid," Dan said.

"Come, come, come. You must have an inkling as to its location. Where do you suspect the cash to be concealed?"

"We don't know exactly," Dan said, "but we think somewhere on the grounds around Wolf Lodge."

Wilbur pushed the sketch toward Dan. "And what does this illustrate?"

"It's a drawing I did of the carvings that are on the fireplace mantle at the lodge. I drew it before the fire. The flames mostly obliterated them."

"Why would Ridgway be inquisitive about them?" Wilbur picked up the paper and scrutinized it. "Why bother to purloin this sketching?"

Dan included Paul in a head nod. "We figured Ridgway was most likely sure of a long stretch in prison for the embezzlement and tax fraud charges. So he set up a trail of clues to lead him to the exact location of where he hid his money. Like a treasure map. We think those marks on the mantle were the first step."

"Have you discerned their meaning?" Wilbur folded the paper and slipped it into his pocket.

Dan hesitated. Gimpy moved the blowtorch flame past Paul, causing him to give a quick cry of pain.

"Okay, stop!" Paul said. "We think the symbols mean you walk about sixty feet from the right side of the lodge's porch. That will bring you to an intersection on a trail. You turn left."

"And?" Wilbur shrugged.

"And we don't know beyond that," Dan said. "When we followed those directions, we discovered an iron spike driven into a tree. We thought there might be other ones, like markers, leading to where Ridgway's cache was, but we're not sure."

"Why did you not pursue your concept?" Wilbur sounded suspicious.

"We beat it out of there fast because somebody started taking potshots at us." Dan glanced between Wilbur and Gimpy.

"Hey, don't look we's two!" Gimpy protested. "If we shoot at somebody, we don't miss."

Wilbur looked toward the roof of the cabin, one finger tapping on his chin. After a few minutes, he checked his watch and stood. "Sunrise occurs in approximately two hours. Gag them again, while we ascertain the veracity of this drawing. We may need to return and request some additional information, depending on the results."

Extinguishing the flame from the blowtorch, Gimpy placed it back on the table, then quickly gagged Dan and Paul. "What if the story is true, and we find the loot? What about them?"

Wilbur opened the door and shrugged. "Well, when the hunters who own this humble abode visit for its next use, they will discover it inhabited by two moldering cadavers." He stepped onto the porch.

Gimpy laughed as he turned down the lantern. "Moldering cadavers," he snickered. "Boy, he sure loves them fancy words." He went out, closing the door behind him. In a few moments, the van drove off.

The inside of the cabin was dark, with shutters over the two windows. A sliver of moonlight made it through the cracks in the wood and outlined objects in the room. The only sounds filling the darkness were the crickets outside and the haunting hoot of an owl.

The brothers broke the deadly stillness of the room with their frenetic efforts, as each desperately sought to free themselves. Dan felt the ropes cutting deeper into his skin as he strained against them, while muffled grunts from across the room suggested that Paul was fighting just as hard. No matter how hard they tried, it seemed like eternity yet the cords would never break. The two brothers stopped their struggles, panting in exhaustion. They were like two small animals tragically caught in a trap that offered no escape.

Moldering cadavers. The words ran through Dan's mind. Then he realized the taut rope under his chest, lashing him to the chair, seemed to have slipped down slightly during his struggle.

With a newfound hope, he started to twist and writhe. He lifted his chest off the chair with his shoulders and pushed forward, the coarse fibers of the rope burning against his skin. With more hard-fought movements, the restraint slowly skittered lower down his torso.

He squirmed and writhed, moved like a belly dancer, sucked in his stomach, until the rope hung limply on his lap. Next, he stretched and grabbed the rope, pulling it around him, until he grasped the knot. He focused on loosening it, his forehead glistening with sweat as he worked at unraveling it. After an age of his fingers pulling and picking, the knot suddenly gave way. An exultant laugh bubbled out of him as he dropped the binding to the floor.

If I can lay my hands on a knife, Dan thought, *I could move towards Paul and cut through the ropes on his wrists. Surely there's one in here. Whoever owns this place must eat meals.*

Dan's gaze darted around the cabin, trying to make out objects out in the dim light. The table was free of any blades, and he didn't spot a drawer to store one. He eventually saw the outline of the only location in the room which might harbor what he needed: a short, two-door cupboard standing against the wall on his right side. He wondered if he could pull the doors of that thing open to check out its contents. It was worth a try.

His ankles were crossed and tied, making it impossible for him to stand up and hop over to the cabinet. Since only one foot could be flat on the floor at a time, he had to crawl across the floorboards.

He maneuvered to the edge of the seat to figure out how to get to the ground. After shifting around a bit, he concluded the only way was, essentially, to topple off.

He pitched himself forward, off the chair, landing hard on his knees. A groan escaped his lips. Paul called to him, a muffled version of "are you okay?" Dan yelled back an equally muffled version of "yes".

After he sized up the cabinet, he realized it would be a slow trip there. Dan started walking on his knees, his bound ankles permitting only tiny baby steps. It must have been a year later by the time he finally reached his goal. He pressed his nose against a knob and twisted, trying to open one door. It jiggled but remained shut fast, so he figured there must be some kind of latch. He had to get the gag off.

He hooked the cloth covering his mouth on the knob. He lifted himself up while working his jaw and lips. The gag dropped around his neck.

"I've got the gag off!" Dan said to Paul. "I'm going to find something to cut these ropes with! At least try to."

He fixed his eyes on the left door as his target. He clamped his teeth on its knob and jerked his head back in one swift motion. The door flew open, and he repeated the feat with the right door, quickly pushing it out of the way with his shoulder. He peered inside.

On the bottom shelf, pots and pans lay piled. The middle shelf had cans of vegetables, fruits, and grains, as well as a bag of flour and a tub of lard. His gaze shifted to the top shelf, just at eye level, and he smiled. He saw metal plates, cups, and one tray filled with forks, spoons, knives, and another that looked like it held cooking utensils.

Eureka! Dan thought. He leaned forward, preparing to grab the tray with his teeth—just like he had done when unlocking the door—but his chin struck the edge of the shelf. He stretched himself as tall as he was able, but still couldn't reach the prize.

Perhaps he could somehow stand, turn around and pull the trays with his hands. He experimented with unique positions until he realized standing upright was out of the question—one wrong move could send him falling over on his side or back, unable to get back to his knees.

Dan sat back and growled in frustration as he glared at the cabinet, now transformed into his mortal enemy. He noticed the shelves weren't locked in place and pegs pushed into the sides of the cupboard held them up. A glimmer of an idea formed in his brain.

He moved himself close to the cupboard, knees touching the wood, then leaned into the cabinet above the cans on the second shelf, the back of his head contacting the backboards. He pushed his head until he felt the bottom of the top shelf. Taking a deep breath, he heaved up and down with all his strength several times. The shelf lifted off its pegs and tilted towards the room. The plates, cups, forks, spoons, utensils, rattled, slid and finally cascaded down his back, clattering as they hit the floor.

"Dan?" Paul asked.

"Okay!" Dan answered. "I found the jackpot!"

Dan sat in the middle of the mess, like a toddler surrounded by his toys. He reached behind him, picking up and discarding items—plates, forks, cups, spoons—that wouldn't be of help. At last he encountered something heavier than the others, a wooden handle worn smooth from years of use. He brushed his little finger along the edge of the knife - it was sharp enough for him to be sure it had been used in a kitchen for slicing vegetables and meats. Success.

"I've got a knife," Dan said. "Here I come!"

He spun on his rear and scooted over to Paul by using his feet. He turned the knife with the blade down while he flattened his back against the side of the bottom bunk. With a deep breath, he let out a slow exhale as he began arching his back to pull himself up onto the mattress. His back and shoulder muscles strained as he lifted his body up slowly on the bunk, inch by inch, like a snake uncoiling itself while at the same time took small hops backwards. With each thrust, he wriggled upward until eventually most of his back was resting on the bed.

"Okay, I'm going to put the knife in your hand. Hang on tight," Dan instructed.

After catching his breath, Dan rolled over on his stomach and used his knees to move next to Paul. He held up the knife to reach for his brother's hand. The two performed an intricate hand ballet as Dan guided the handle into Paul's waiting palm. When Paul's grip became secure, he grunted.

Dan contorted his body and raised his wrists, pressing the ropes into contact with the blade. His arms and shoulders bulged with effort as he moved them back and forth rhythmically, sawing away at the tough cords. Finally, one strand snapped, followed by the second. Dan tugged, and his hands broke free.

"Almost done." Dan took the knife from Paul and cut the cords tying his ankles and stood awkwardly. "My feet are numb, like they're asleep." He stomped the floor a few times. "Okay, my dear brother, now it's your turn."

Dan sliced the ropes binding Paul to the bedpost and his wrists. Paul sat on the mattress as Dan dropped to one knee to start work on freeing his brother's feet.

"I take a size 10," Paul said after pulling off the gag.

"Well, you're in luck, sir. We have a lovely pair of black patent leather loafers that may fit you," Dan said.

"With tassels?"

"Why, yes, of course. Tassels are very in." Dan threw the ropes aside and stood, tossing the knife on the top bunk. He gazed at Paul with a grin. "Man, the way you stared down that blowtorch..."

Paul returned the grin as he rubbed his wrists and got up. "And you performed an excellent impersonation of a trained seal yourself. A rather smart one, at that."

"Where's my fish?" Dan imitated a seal's bark, and he clapped his arms together like flippers. The two laughed a little too hard to release their tension. "Let's hike back to the highway and see if that good-lookin' mug of yours can induce a lovely young lady to give us a ride back into town. Or hitch a lift in a truck full of chickens, whichever passes by first. Then we'll call the sheriff to report our own kidnapping."

After Paul retrieved his glasses, the brothers left the cabin, emerging onto the road which ended in front of it, little more than just two tracks in the dirt. They started following it. After a few minutes of walking in silence, Paul spoke.

"Dan, what about Dad?" Paul asked hesitantly, almost as though not wanting an answer.

"What...what about him?"

"What they said about him, in there. About Dad being a member of Rizzo's gang."

Dan was quiet for a moment, trying to grapple with the implications of the words he had heard in the cabin. "I'm not sure...I mean, we look like Dad. Everybody has always told us that. They seemed to have known him. Mom and Dad came from Chicago...but that's all we really know about their past. No stories about their growing up, or our grandparents, other than they have passed away. We've never seen photos, school yearbooks..."

He hesitated before he continued. "I suppose they got their high school diplomas from night school in Belmont, when we were babies. That's what they said, right? Maybe it means nothing. That would explain why they don't have any yearbooks like we do and..." Dan's voice trailed off. He didn't want to accept what the Daltons had said about the twin's father, but his mind kept running over what little he knew of their parents. "I guess it is possible Dad had some kind of..." He fumbled for a word. "...connection with Rizzo when he was younger."

They reached an intersection with another dirt road and stopped.

"Now where do we go?" Paul looked both directions.

"When the van left the highway, it turned right, right, left, so we go that way." Dan indicated the direction they should take. The two set off. He had hoped the new route would provide a distraction, so he could avoid talking more about their father, but it wasn't.

"We could ask Mom," Paul ventured.

Dan shook his head. "It could bring up some terrible memories. I don't want to put her through that."

"No, neither do I," Paul said.

"They were secretive about their backgrounds for a reason." Dan sorted through his conflicted feelings. "Honestly, Paul, I don't know if I really want to know the truth." He struggled to assemble his thoughts into words. "Listen, our dad was a good man. He worked hard to provide for us, to raise us right. His being in a gang with bootleggers...it doesn't fit with the man we knew...the one we want to remember, the one we admire. The dad we love. Maybe it's best to leave the past in the past."

"What if it comes up because of this business?"

"Then our job is to stand behind Mom, period," Dan stated.

"Agreed."

As they made the third crossroad, the darkness gradually gave way to the faint pink light of dawn. The silhouettes of trees slowly became clearer and more distinct, their branches reaching out to the morning sky.

Paul stopped. "Wait. Do you recognize where we are?"

Dan looked around. "Aren't we—"

"On the road to the quarry," Paul confirmed. "The Daltons broke into one of the hunters' cabins that are tucked into the woods in this area."

"That saves us from a hitch!" Dan said. "We'll go past the quarry, continue to Wolf Lodge, and then go down to the resort. We can call the sheriff from there."

"What about the Daltons?" Paul asked. "They'll be in the area around the lodge, following the directions from the mantle carvings. I don't hanker to run into them twice in one day."

"Neither do I, but we know the forest there better than they do," Dan said. "And I'm sure they'll be plowing through the woods like a couple of elephants. It'll be easy to outflank them."

They slowly made their way up the winding dirt road, Dan in the lead. He realized he had been up all night, and fatigue was weighing on him like an anchor. A glance toward Paul showed he was just as tired.

The brothers let out a sigh when tall pine trees came into view, which stood at the crest of the hill. As they rounded the curve, they stopped in their tracks. Parked in front of a jumble of boulders that marked the dead end was a red Mercury convertible with its top down.

"Isn't that the one Waxton tried to sell us?" Paul pointed to it. "A fancy car to drive up here to fish."

Dan didn't answer for a moment as he stared at it. "Perhaps it's not here for fishing," he mumbled. He walked toward the convertible, Paul following.

When he got to the passenger side, he glanced cautiously around.

Then, quickly sticking his arm inside, he opened the glove box.

"What are you doing?" Paul hissed in some alarm.

"I'm playing on a hunch. I want to check the registration," Dan said as he pulled out the paperwork and read it. He nodded. "Just as I thought. The registered owner of this fine vehicle is one Edward Ridgway."

Chapter Sixteen

"Ridgway!" Paul checked the document over Dan's shoulder.

"He even registered it to our address." Dan pointed to the line.

"The nerve of some people." Paul shaded his eyes with one hand and examined the woods. "So Ridgway and the Daltons are all roaming around out there. Things ought to get interesting if they smack into each other. It'll sound like the opening day of hunting season." He tapped the fender. "Why two cars?"

Dan stuffed the paperwork back in the glove compartment. "He probably got wise to the Daltons knowing about the Hudson, and after his escapades at our house, maybe us, too. So he needed something else, although a red convertible is a little flashy. Let's see if the trunk is open." He walked to the rear of the car and pushed the button. The lid popped up. "Well, no luggage, but here's a box." He opened the top cardboard flap. "My painting! Hey, its backing is loose."

Paul checked the front of the carton. "There's a shipping label stuck on the front...addressed to Ridgway in Mexico City. Well, we know who your art patron is."

Dan slammed the lid shut and stepped back. "I don't think it's my artwork he wants, as much as it pains me to admit it." He thought for a moment. "How about this? Because of his work with Rizzo, Ridgway is well-versed in the banks, fences, smugglers and anybody else who could help him get his money out of the country. But he's too cagey to trust a single channel with the whole wad, so he's spreading his loot among multiple ways to get it to Mexico. That includes my painting. He takes a stack of bills, hides them behind my picture, seals the cardboard backing over them, and sends off my artwork as if it were just any ordinary parcel."

"And here I thought your art wouldn't amount to anything," Paul said. "Do you think we should wait here or hunt him down?"

"I don't want to chance meeting that group of armed merry men in the woods, especially Ridgway. He surprised us out there once already." Dan reopened the glove compartment and fished out the registration. He folded it and slipped it into his hip pocket. "I'll just hang on to this. It'll have all the information the police need to set up a roadblock. We'll stay here until he leaves, then—"

Paul grabbed Dan and pulled him down behind the car. "Check out the hut," he said in a quiet voice.

Dan peered cautiously over the top of the trunk. The door of the metal shack opened and Ridgway stepped out, lugging two large buckets. He put one on the ground and took the second to the far side of the quarry. With quick, efficient movements, he shifted out its dirt contents over a wide area, mixing it into the soil with his scuffed shoes. He returned to the first bucket. He pulled out rocks of all sizes, scattering them across the floor of the quarry. When his task was complete, he hoisted both pails and trudged back to the hut.

"What's all that about?" Paul asked. "What's he doing in there?"

"I don't know, but we should find out." Dan glanced around. He pointed to where part of the quarry wall had collapsed in a landslide. "Let's skirt the rim and go down by the rocks over there. They'll give us cover."

The brothers dropped into a crouch and scurried to the area. They picked their way down the slope, balancing on jagged stones and slabs of granite. Dan and Paul made their descent as silently as possible, wincing each time a foot kicked a stone, sending it tumbling into the pit below. They held their breath, straining to listen for any sign Ridgway had heard them. The door to the hut remained closed. When they reached the bottom, they huddled behind a boulder and peered around the edge.

The shed was small, the corrugated metal siding and roof dull gray and weather-beaten, with rust stains streaking down the walls. It was built in a lean-to style, hard against the face of the cliff. Next to the door was a window.

"Ah, the window is so dirty it's like a wall. No way to see in," Dan said.

"Look, at the back where the shack meets the rock." Paul pointed. "There's a gap between the side and the roof."

"Yeah, but it's pretty high—" Dan slapped Paul's arm with the back of his hand. "I got it. We'll do what we did in the pump house. You know, you sit on my shoulders, then you can check inside."

Paul smiled, and he raised his thumb in the air. The two hurried to the corner of the hut, wedged against the rocky cliff. Dan got down on his knees and Paul clambered onto his brother's shoulders, locking his legs around Dan's chest for support. With one swift motion, Dan grabbed hold of Paul's shins and stood tall as Paul used the rocks to steady himself.

Dan turned and shuffled to the wall. He looked up. Dan squinted through the opening and shook his head. He pressed his left foot into Dan's chest twice. Dan took a few steps in that direction and stopped. Paul shook his head once more.

"Am I in time for the next performance of the Case Twins' Acrobatic Troupe?"

Startled, Dan spun to the sound of the voice. Ridgway stood by the shed's corner, holding a gun with the calm assurance of somebody well acquainted with its use and operation. The barrel pointed directly at Dan's midsection.

"I guess you didn't make it to your brother's place," Dan said.

Ridgway chuckled flatly. "No. Something came up, so I had to change my plans." He motioned with the revolver. "If you came to see the inside, I'd be delighted to give you a guided tour. Get down and put your hands on your heads."

Dan got down on one knee and Dan climbed off.

"This just isn't our day," Paul sighed. He put his hands on his head.

"I guess I can be glad it isn't a burlap bag," Dan replied as he complied with Ridgway's command.

"Young men are prone to perform rash acts, like trying to rush me to grab the gun," Ridgway said, "but I wouldn't suggest it. Be advised I'm quite an excellent shot. I'd get at least one of you."

"Like out in the woods?" Paul said. "You missed twice."

"I meant to," Ridgway answered. "Sometimes it takes more skill not to hit a target."

"By the way," Dan said, "did you set up that business with the well?"

"Of course, but I intended it for the Daltons. Unfortunately, they're too stupid even to fall into a trap." Ridgway stepped back and waved the gun. "Inside."

The twins walked around the corner of the shed to the door.

"Use your foot and open the door all the way. Make it touch the wall," Ridgway directed. "Walk forward until I tell you to halt. Remain there with your hands on your heads and backs to the door."

Dan pushed the door, then he and Paul stepped inside until Ridgway commanded, "Stop!" As they halted, the light from outside diminished as the door closed behind them.

"You may put your hands down. Turn to face me," Ridgway said.

It took Dan a few moments for his eyes to adjust to the dark interior. A small amount of sunlight filtered through the filthy window as well as the gaps around the door, outlining Ridgway's figure as he leaned against it. The cramped shed contained only some tools in one corner and the two buckets Dan had seen earlier. He looked in back of himself. The rock wall held the low entrance to a cave.

"Charming, don't you think, Dan?" Paul commented.

"Very homey," Dan observed. "It just needs some finishing touches."

"This was originally used to store explosives when the quarry was in operation. They kept the actual dynamite in the cave," Ridgway said. "At least, the woman at the historical society told me that."

"Mrs. Campbell knows her local history," Dan said.

"Of course, when Lorenzo Rizzo owned the lodge, it was for liquor storage," Ridgway said. "He also planned to extend the cave to the basement of the house. It was to be a handy escape route if the casino ever received an unannounced visit by federal agents. The work actually started, but ended when Rizzo found himself ended by his rivals."

"Fascinating," Paul said, "but why tell us?"

"I'm sure he'll give a reason soon," Dan returned.

"You are correct," Ridgway said. "The new tunnel didn't reach too far back and wasn't well-braced. It collapsed several years ago. I have been spending the last several exhausting nights digging it out, but now I have two strapping, strong teenagers to finish the task."

"But why dig..." Dan stopped as the picture came clear, like fog evaporating off a landscape. He faced Ridgway and applauded.

"What...what's that all about?" Paul demanded.

"Because, my dear brother, a master has played us like a pair of violins." Dan gestured toward Ridgway, who smiled and bowed his head in acknowledgment. Dan jerked his thumb at the cave. "The money is back there. The lodge had nothing to do with it. Never did." Dan addressed Ridgway. "Let me see if I got this straight. When your embezzlement scheme—"

"Please! 'Scheme'. That's such an ugly word," Ridgway said.

"But accurate," Dan noted. "Your scheme collapsed because of the Superior Brewery audit. Most likely, your first instinct was to grab as much of the funds as possible and take off. But living the life of a fugitive, even as a wealthy one, would make an unpleasant future. You know, always having to look over your shoulder, that sort of thing. Instead, you played the long game. You stashed your, um, 'proceeds'," Dan waved toward the cave entrance, "back there in cash. That ensured the money couldn't be frozen in bank accounts, or tracked unless serial numbers were kept or the bills were marked, which, of course, they weren't. You got arrested, tried, and served your time. Why go through all the trouble? Why put yourself through that? Simple. You knew you'd have a three hundred-thousand-dollar payday—tax free—after your release from prison. Am I correct?"

Ridgway nodded. "You are."

"He reads a lot of detective magazines," Paul put in.

"While in jail, you most likely used your time productively, researching foreign countries that weren't too fussy about the source of a resident's wealth," Dan said.

"The prison had an excellent library." Ridgway smiled.

"After you got out, you laid low until finally deciding it was time to retrieve the money," Dan went on. "You made reservations at the resort. But your plans leaked somehow, and on the trip here you discovered Archer was tailing you. So you got off the bus at the gas station, pretended to re-board with the idea of hitching a ride in town instead, then getting the bus the next morning. Although Wilbur didn't believe me, our meeting at the Wayside was completely a coincidence. I thought your surprised reaction when you saw us was because we're identical twins. That happens a lot. Now I know the real reason was our resemblance to our father."

"It is striking," Ridgway confirmed.

"On the way to Farmingford, we were passed by the black van," Dan said, "and you spotted the Daltons in it. That put you on notice they were also following as well."

Ridgway dismissed the idea with a wave of his hand. "I already knew that, since they are not the most subtle of people, but that is a minor point."

"You spent the night in town, spreading around the 'brother in Nebraska' story, making sure people understood you were continuing your journey. Meanwhile, Archer, and I assume the Daltons, found out you weren't on the bus, so they returned to Farmingford. You may have even passed them coming this way while you were traveling to Belmont."

"I did. It was quite amusing."

"Your pursuers wasted at least one day backtracking you. When in Belmont, you picked up your original plan, bought the Hudson and drove out to the resort to check in. You hiked over here, somehow getting inside..." Dan gestured around the shack.

"Duplicate padlock keys are easy to obtain," Ridgway gave a half-shrug and a confident smile, "if you know the right people."

"However, you ran into a big problem: the cave-in." Dan continued as he thought out loud. "That meant retrieving your money would take longer than expected. The more time to reach the cash, the more likely Archer or the Daltons would pick up your trail again." He leaned toward his brother. "This is where we came in."

"Oh, goodie. I was wondering where we did," Paul remarked.

"We served as decoys to draw the Daltons' attention away from him and put it on us, giving him more time to work alone. He could only dig here at night without being spotted, and wanted the Daltons to waste their time dealing with us." Dan turned to Ridgway. "That's the reason I saw the curtains at your cottage closed during the day: you were sleeping."

Ridgway nodded, amused. He gestured to Dan to continue.

"You figured if you recognized us as our dad's sons, the Daltons would too, and seeing the three of us together in our jeep tightened the connection. After you awoke from your night's labors, you used the day planting clues and hints leading the Daltons to conclude we were working with you. Or we were after the money on our own. Either angle would fit your plans. I also suppose you figured they would think we were easier to follow."

"And, um, easier to 'persuade' to give them information," Paul added.

"Yes," Ridgway agreed. "They were quite infamous for their methods of extracting information. I'm glad you survived."

"Very thoughtful of you," Paul said.

"Don't mention it," Ridgway returned.

Dan went on. "So just as a magician uses misdirection to distract the audience from how the trick works, Wolf Lodge became the supposed hiding place of your cache. As part of your plan, you followed us to the library that day, trailed by the Daltons, of course. You went inside to make it look like we were holding a cozy little meeting. How am I doing so far?"

"Very good," Ridgway approved. "On my first day, I hiked over here to check the condition of my, shall we say, vault? On my way here, I spotted your brother and his girlfriend at the beach. I assume he noticed me and called you, because when I was returning after the disheartening discovery of the cave-in, I saw you prowling around the lodge. That's when I thought of the distraction: plant the notion I stashed the money in the ruins, and get the Daltons to fall for it. The carvings on the mantle, made by a drunk gambler year ago, came to mind."

He laughed at the memory. "Rizzo was furious when he found out—yelled he 'didn't run no cheap roadhouses'—but it gave me the idea. Cryptic clues leading to a treasure, perhaps hidden in an abandoned house...the stuff of many a mystery story!"

"So the day I followed you to the lodge—" Dan started.

"The day I *led* you to the lodge, you mean," Ridgway corrected.

"Granted. By the way, what did you clobber me with?"

"A blackjack." Ridgway grinned. "I liked the touch of pulling down the wall on top of you. It added to the intrigue."

Dan nodded. "Lovely gesture. So the creel, the paper, leaving the pencil...the point of all that, along with the lump on my head, was to suggest the money was hidden in the building."

"But then I realized I couldn't continue with the deception because I didn't know your father's—Slick's—real name," Ridgway said. "You see, in Rizzo's organization—"

"Names were not important," Paul finished. "Yes, yes, we know."

"I recalled you telling me you did work for the historical society, so I took a trip to the museum. I purchased your painting…you are an excellent artist, by the way."

"Thank you." Dan shot a glance at his brother. "Although some wonder what my artwork will amount to."

"Hey, I'm a boxer," Paul shrugged. "What do I know of art?"

"Your signature gave me your name, and the phone book, your address," Ridgway said. "At my prodding, Mrs. Campbell also showed me some sketches you did of the interior of Wolf Lodge. It gave me an idea, leading to my nighttime visit to your house."

"Staged to make it appear to the Daltons you were double-crossing us, because we had uncovered an important clue to the money's location?" Dan suggested.

Ridgway nodded. "Precisely. Your drawing of the mantle carvings fit the ruse perfectly."

"How did you find us in the forest?" Paul asked.

"That was pure luck." Ridgway chuckled. "I was returning from my night's labors and stumbled upon you two. A few shots at you deepened the riddle of the hidden cash."

"What about the two cars?" Dan questioned.

Ridgway smiled. "Your father was a bright lad. That's why Rizzo took such a liking to him. I'm sure you can figure it out."

"Your stay ended at the resort, and you couldn't extend it because the place is completely reserved, so you moved to the Midway…" Dan thought for a moment. "The Hudson must have been another decoy, but…"

"You are partly accurate," Ridgway responded. "I made a booking for two rooms at the motel and drove the Hudson there. Obviously, the Daltons and you, presumably, both followed me. I climbed out of one room's bathroom window in the rear, walked to the diner, and hitched a ride into town with an accommodating insurance salesman."

"Back in Farmingford, you purchased the convertible from Waxton," Dan said. "He must have loved making the sale."

"Oh, he did, particularly since I didn't dicker on the price." Ridgway smiled. "I returned to the motel. I had requested my second room be far away from the highway—I told the manager my friend I reserved the room for had insomnia—and stayed in that one. Now and then I would use the bathroom window to leave the second room and go back to the first, so my tails could see me in the original one."

"Brilliant. Your reputation is well deserved," Dan said.

"Now it is my turn to thank you," Ridgway said. "Now, are all the ends tied up nice and neat? Is everything tidy? No loose threads?"

Dan and Paul exchanged glances and nodded.

"Splendid. Now to work." Ridgway gestured to the cave. "It is daylight, and you'll need to hurry. Fortunately, there is only a little farther to dig. You may begin."

Paul took a step toward the tools.

"Stop!" Ridgway ordered. He waved Paul back with his gun.

"But we need something to dig with," Paul said.

"You can employ shovels as weapons," Ridgway responded. "You will use your hands. Oh, and should you decide to throw rocks at me, remember a bullet travels faster. Start." His thumb pulled back on the gun's hammer. "Now."

Chapter Seventeen

The twins looked at each other.

Paul bowed and held out one hand. "After you."

"No, no, I insist," Dan replied, "after you."

They stooped and entered the low opening. After a few steps, it became clear that crawling on their hands and knees would be easier.

"You will find a battery-powered lantern when you get to the back," Ridgway said as they moved away.

Dan and Paul felt their way forward in the dark, dank air. They made a sharp left turn and the two of them scooted ahead, following an increasingly narrow passageway until they reached a barricade of rocks. Paul leaned to one side and ran his fingers along the cool surface.

"Here's the lantern," he said. There was a slight click, then the cave was bathed in stark white light. He viewed the wall of rubble in front of them. "How are we supposed to clear this with just our hands?" he yelled back to Ridgway.

"I already told you," came the tart reply. "The two of you are young and strong. The faster you start your task, the sooner you finish."

"Sounds like Mom telling us to clean our rooms." Paul gritted his teeth and heaved a rock out of the way with a loud, angry grunt. Dan joined, and the two strained against the dirt and rubble, filling the area with muted thuds as rocks cracked and puffs of dust settled around them. Rivulets of perspiration ran down their faces and bodies, leaving mud-streaked trails in their wake.

Without being able to use the buckets, they stacked the stones and dirt along the sides of the passageway behind them. As Dan rolled a large stone into position, an ominous thud shook the walls, followed by a sharp blast of air. He gasped and tried to stifle his coughs as he squinted through the suffocating cloud of gray. With dread, he looked back—Paul's legs protruded from beneath a mound of rubble.

"Paul!"

"What happened back there?" called Ridgway.

"Cave-in!" Dan shouted, his voice shaking as he dug with his hands, throwing rocks and stones behind him. Sweat beaded on his forehead and his breaths came in ragged gasps. He uncovered Paul's back. Dan took hold of his legs and yanked. With a last tug, he pulled his brother's head from under the remaining dirt and rocks. Dan grabbed Paul's shoulders and shook him gently. "Paul? Paul? Are you alright?"

Paul coughed and groaned as he raised his head from the ground, his glasses coated in dust. He met Dan's gaze with a crooked grin. He pulled his hands out from under the dirt that still covered them. They were gripping a metal cash box.

"We got it!" Dan called.

"You mean, *I've* got it." Paul removed his glasses and blew the dust off them.

Dan grinned. "Paul's got it!"

"I don't care who has it!" Excitement tinged Ridgway's voice. "Just bring it out here immediately!"

"You heard what the man said." Dan cocked his head toward the opening of the cave.

"Immediately, he says," Paul mocked.

The two squirmed their way back down the passage, kicking and pushing the rocks out of their way. They reached the mouth of the cave.

"Stay there, on your hands and knees!" Ridgway ordered. "Where is it? Well, where is it?" Paul held up the box. Ridgway's face broke into a smug smile of victory. "After all those years, after what I endured in prison...at last I get my reward. Put it on the floor and slide it to me." Paul did so, and Ridgway patted the box as though it were a long-lost pet. "You may come out into the room."

The brothers did, standing at the mouth of the cave. Ridgway chuckled.

"You two look like miners," he said. "Now, if you don't mind, I need you to remove your belts."

"Our belts?" Paul echoed.

"Yes, those leather straps you wear around your waist," Ridgway sarcastically replied.

Dan unfastened his belt. "I think, my dear brother, we're about to be tied up again. Twice within twenty-four hours. That must be a new world record."

"I bet this doesn't happen in the detective stories you read." Paul unbuckled his belt.

"No, it's not believable. But fiction isn't real life." Dan removed his belt and allowed it to dangle freely in his hand, the weighty buckle at the bottom swaying back and forth.

Ridgway held the revolver pointed at the boys, his hand steady. "I suggest you drop your belts on the ground and don't think of using them to attack me. Otherwise, I'll have to use a more permanent method of stopping you." The two did as they were told, and Ridgway gestured to Paul with his gun. "You! Lie face down on the floor. And you," he pointed at Dan, "tie his hands together behind him with his belt."

Paul lay down on the floor. Dan got on one knee and looped the belt around his brother's wrists.

Ridgway shifted his position to observe the operation, his revolver aimed at Paul's back. "Tightly—can't you pull it harder?"

"Sorry, buddy," Dan said as he tightened the bonds.

Paul winced. "Don't worry about it."

"All right," Ridgway commanded Dan. "Now tie your belt in a loose knot and lie face down there next to your brother. Put your hands behind your back and slip them through the belt."

Dan obeyed, the leather belt creaking as he knotted it loosely. He lay down on the floor, chest pressing against the hard surface, and slipped his wrists through the belt.

Ridgway leaned over Dan. "Try nothing. I still have the gun pointed at you." The belt cinched tighter around Dan's wrists, biting into his skin. Ridgway stood upright. "Now just remain calm and quiet for an hour. I really don't want to harm Slick's children."

"I'm certainly glad to hear that," Dan fired back.

Ridgway's soft chuckle echoed in the tiny room. As he picked up the heavy cash box, it scraped across the floor with a chilling sound. His footsteps tapped as he made his way to the door. It creaked open and then closed with a muffled thud.

Immediately, the brothers sat up and moved back to back. Their fingers grappled with the belts.

"No, no, this time, let me do the honors." Paul gripped the knot around Dan's wrists and began to work it loose. "All of Rizzo's gang must have earned merit badges in knot tying," he said through clenched teeth. The belt loosened around Dan's wrists. "There! Got it!"

"We're getting good at being escape artists. Better than Harry Houdini." Dan started undoing the knot binding Paul's hands together.

Outside, the convertible's engine roared to life. "Hurry! He's going to get away!" Paul cried.

"He can't make a fast getaway on that road. If he tries, he'll end up with a flat tire or a broken axle." Dan freed Paul's hands.

The moment Paul was loose, he shot up and ran to the door. Dan gathered the belts and hurried after him. Paul grabbed the doorknob and tugged on it. It didn't budge.

"Of course it's locked," Dan sighed. "What else would we expect?"

Paul uttered a wordless cry of rage as he grabbed a shovel and shattered the window. He used the blade to scrape away any remaining jagged pieces, then threw the tool aside. He clambered out of the opening, followed closely by Dan. The convertible was no longer visible, but they could hear its motor as the car picked its way down the potholed road.

"We can cut him off at the switchbacks!" Paul sprinted toward one side of the quarry. With the alacrity of a monkey, he started to scale the rocky wall. Dan trailed behind, climbing slower.

Dan had only made it two-thirds of the way up by the time Paul reached the crest and disappeared from sight. Dan quickly scrambled up to the top and took in his surroundings. Ridgway's car was slowly weaving around a tight bend in the distance while Paul was running to the edge of the next switchback's banking. Dan wasted no time setting off after him.

Paul yanked Dan behind a cluster of bushes when he caught up with him. The two perched atop a steep slope that was roughly ten feet above the dirt road. Paul grabbed Dan by the shoulder and pointed. The convertible rounded the curve and bounced down on the uneven surface toward them.

"Now what?" Dan asked.

Paul didn't respond, but took off his glasses and handed them to his brother.

"Wait, Paul...what...what do you have in mind?"

Paul's answer was a move into a crouched position as the car drew nearer.

Dan realized what his brother's plan was. "Paul, no—"

He didn't have a chance to finish his sentence. The car reached just below them, and Paul suddenly launched himself into the air. He flew off the edge of the steep bank, landing with a thud in the back seat of the convertible. Ridgway yelped, maintaining his grip on the steering wheel with one hand while rapidly reaching for Paul with the other.

Paul dodged his grasp and lunged for the gun lying on the front seat. Ridgway also made a grab for the revolver, and the two fought for its possession. During the struggle, Ridgway's foot pressed down on the accelerator. The car shot forward, then veered off the road, the right front tilting into a ditch. The left rear tire hung in the air, spinning uselessly.

Dan half scrambled and half fell down the embankment and ran for the convertible. The revolver wrenched loose of Ridgway's and Paul's grip. It flew free and landed on the ground almost at Dan's feet. He scooped it up.

Ridgway grunted and shoved Paul away. He stumbled out of the car, but Paul was too fast—he leapt forward and tackled Ridgway to the ground. They grappled in the road's dirt, rolling over and over. With one swift move, Paul snaked his right arm around Ridgway's neck. Heaving with every ounce of strength, he arched his body and got Ridgway off-balance enough to flip him onto his back. Straddling his opponent, Paul delivered two hard punches to his jaw. With a groan, Ridgway went limp. Paul stood as Dan ran to his side.

"Excuse me mister, you seemed to have dropped these." Dan handed Paul his glasses. He looked down at Ridgway. "I guess I'm too late to be of assistance. Not that you needed any."

Paul chuckled as he put on his glasses. "My first knockout."

Dan hoisted Paul's right hand over his head. "And the new world's cham-peen!" he called out. He held out their belts. "I brought them along so we wouldn't be embarrassed if our pants dropped around our ankles, but we know they have other uses."

Paul grinned in agreement, and they tied Ridgway's hands and feet with the belts, leaving him on the ground. Dan grabbed Paul's arm.

"Hear that?"

Paul nodded. "Another motor."

Dan peered through the trees to the lower road. A black delivery van was working its way up the switchbacks. "The Daltons!"

He rushed to the car and picked up the cash box, balancing it on the convertible's hood. After looking around, he gestured to the shrubs lining the road. "There's the bait. Get a weapon. Hide in the bushes. When the Daltons stop, we'll jump them."

Paul dashed to the trunk of the convertible, yanked open the lid, and grabbed the tire iron. He jogged back to the front. Dan motioned for him to go behind a clump of shrubs on the left side of the road. Dan scrambled across the dirt and positioned himself concealed in another cluster of branches on the opposite edge.

Dan's grip on the gun tightened and loosened in a nervous rhythm. He mentally prepared for what he may have to do, questioning if he had the courage to use a weapon against another person. The van's engine roar grew louder as it struggled up the steep incline.

The van stopped on the other side of the bush. The motor switched off. Dan jumped out.

"Now!" he shouted and squeezed the trigger. A single bullet shot from the revolver and pierced the radiator of the van. Hissing white steam erupted, filling the air around them. Paul rushed out, swinging his tire iron and shattering the windshield with one powerful blow, the glass fracturing in a chaotic pattern of thin spider web cracks. The Daltons instinctively held their arms over their faces to protect themselves from the shattering glass.

"Hands on top of the dashboard!" Dan hollered. "Do it now!"

After a confused look between them, the Daltons did what they were told.

"You, Wilbur, take your gun by its handle with two fingers of your left hand, and toss it out the window. And please don't claim you're not armed. I won't believe you." Dan leveled the gun. "I should mention Slick took us deer hunting. Don't make me imagine a pair of antlers sprouting out of your head."

Wilbur, sitting in the passenger's seat, took his left hand and reached into his right coat pocket. He pulled out a revolver and threw it out of the van. Dan moved over, picked it up, and slipped it into his waistband.

"Same for you, Gimpy," Dan called.

Gimpy tossed his gun out the driver's window.

Paul retrieved it and let the tire iron fall to the dirt. After a second, he took off his glasses and held them out toward his twin while he stared at Gimpy. "Dan."

Dan took the glasses while he kept the cab covered with the gun.

"Gimpy, I believe my brother wishes to have a friendly conversation with you."

"But he's got a gun!" Gimpy whined.

Paul dropped the gun to the dirt and kicked it to Dan.

"Not anymore." Dan picked up the revolver. "I have three, in case you're keeping count."

Paul took a couple of steps back. He waved his hands, motioning Gimpy to get out. After a glance to Wilbur, Gimpy opened the door of the van. He stepped out, jaw clenched, fists raised. A challenging sneer spread across his lips when he saw Paul.

Wasting no time, Paul unleashed a flurry of blows. Gimpy staggered back, surprised at their force. But he quickly regained his composure and fought back. The two traded punches, each of them taking hits and delivering them.

Dan watched with fascination as the battle intensified, as though watching two strangers. He'd seen his brother in the ring before, but never saw him fight like this. It was like Paul transformed into a wild beast, all primal instinct and raw power.

Gimpy threw a solid punch to Paul's jaw, and Dan winced. But Paul merely grunted and shook his head, then lunged forward and landed a punch of his own. Gimpy stumbled, then regained his balance and came at Paul again. The two circled each other warily, then Paul feinted a left and jabbed a crushing blow to Gimpy's stomach.

With a gasp, Gimpy doubled over. Paul took the flat palm of one hand and brought it up strong against Gimpy's chin. Gimpy's head snapped back. He stumbled backwards a few steps, then dropped to the dirt unconscious. Paul stood over him, panting. He held up two fingers to Dan.

Dan moved to his brother's side, keeping Wilbur covered. "Well, that was...most impressive. But even I know that last punch wasn't regulation."

Paul grinned as he took his glasses and put them on. "Don't tell the ref."

Dan addressed Wilbur. "You. Get out and take your brother to the back of the van."

"But he is heavy," Wilbur complained.

"I do not care." Dan waved the revolver. "Do it."

Wilbur slipped out of the door. He grabbed Gimpy's arms and began to drag him to the rear of the van, groaning and swearing.

Dan supervised the operation, gun in hand. "Get those doors open in the back," he told Paul.

Paul took the keys out of the ignition and had the van's back doors swung wide by the time Wilbur reached them with his burden.

"Inside," Dan ordered.

With more grunting and complaining, Wilbur heaved Gimpy into the cargo area. Paul locked the doors. The twins looked at each other.

"Dad took us deer hunting? Since when?" Paul cocked an eyebrow.

"Well, I had to say something. I didn't want the Daltons to know I've never held a gun before." Dan shrugged. "The only lie I've told in my sterling life."

Paul coughed. "I could reel off a few that have crossed your lips, Saint Dan. Since you're armed, I'll hike over to the resort and call the sheriff." He gestured toward Ridgway. "We'll drag him closer so you can keep watch on all our trophies."

"Of course." Dan clapped Paul on the back. "You really are something, you know that?"

"So are you. We make a pretty damn good team." Paul grinned. "But we always have, my dear brother, we always have." He turned to leave, then stopped. "You realize Mom gets back tomorrow, don't you?"

"Yes."

"Do you remember what we promised to her if she let us stay by ourselves?" Paul folded his arms.

"You mean to keep out of trouble while she's out of town?"

"Exactly. So which one of us is going to tell her about all this?" Paul gestured toward the van.

The twins pointed to each other and spoke at the same time. "You are."

****

"Ten thousand dollars!"

Dan and Paul's mother stared at the telegram she held. She was in her mid-thirties, attractive, with black eyes and hair. The twins, dressed in their best suits, stood in front of her. The three were in the small park situated across the street from the Belmont train station.

Although Mrs. Case was slender, she usually projected a no-nonsense, even tough, strength at the same time. But that failed her as she read Ridgway's name. She turned pale and sank down on the bench as she finished the telegram. The twins took seats on either side of her. "Eddie Ridgway!"

"We also met the Dalton brothers," Dan added. His mother gasped and looked at him, her eyes full of fear and anxiety. Dan grinned. "Don't worry. Paul took care of Ridgway and Gimpy Dalton. He knocked them both out cold."

Mrs. Case chuckled. She patted Paul's hand and smiled approvingly. "Good for you. They deserve it."

"Are you ready to hear the full story now?" Dan asked.

His mother took a deep, shuddering breath and nodded. She listened to her sons tell of their experiences, blinking away the tears that threatened, flinching at times, her gaze fixed on the cracks in the sidewalk. When they finished, she opened her arms to both of them and held them tightly, not saying a word. The three of them sat together on a bench for a few minutes, no one willing to break the quiet.

"Your father and I met when we were fifteen," Mrs. Case started softly. "He ran numbers for Rizzo while I worked in one of his speakeasies, a bar. I was a...hostess, shall we call it? Rizzo kept promoting your dad, but he never took part in any of the rough stuff. I want you both to know that. It's important. None of the rough stuff. He refused."

Dan and Paul nodded.

"Rizzo moved your dad higher and higher in his organization, finally giving him the responsibility of overseeing liquor shipments and planning the routes for the trucks." She chuckled bitterly. "It was almost like a legitimate business. However, Rizzo wanted your father as one of his top deputies. That meant being involved in more unsavory operations, like narcotics. Your dad didn't want that, but nobody walked out on Lorenzo Rizzo. Ever."

Mrs. Case sat back on the hard bench. "That day in June was hot. Humid, sticky, miserable. Rizzo and his crew—your dad included—had gone to one warehouse. Frankie McFarlane had set up a trap with a line of men waiting to ambush them. In an instant, fourteen people died from bullets flying–but not fifteen. Your father jumped out a window before it was too late. He showed up at my apartment later that night, cut up and smeared with blood. He scared the life out of me, the way he looked.

As I nursed him back to health, we decided the massacre was an opportunity given to us...by fate, or God, or random chance. A chance to change our lives, to become better than what we had settled for. I know it sounds like something from a movie, but we saw a possibility to start over.

Your dad had heard Rizzo talk about the Farmingford area, and it sounded to us like a lovely spot to raise a family. And we figured nobody from the old gang would dare come near because of its association with Rizzo. Neither of us had a police record—just lucky, I suppose—so we didn't have to worry about that. We eloped and moved here. You two came soon after."

"So your love changed Dad," Paul said.

"No, no." The twin's mother smiled. It was radiant. "Our love changed each other."

Dan and Paul stood, faced their mother, and held out their hands. She grasped them, and they helped her to her feet. The brothers bowed.

"And now, Mr. Paul Case and I request the pleasure of your company for a steak dinner at Sandy's Fine Dining. Our treat," Dan said.

"You can tell us all that is new in the wonderful world of water management," Paul added.

"We promise to listen with rapt attention," Dan put in.

Mrs. Case laughed and smiled at her sons. "I cannot think of two more exceptional young men to be my escorts."

The three linked arms and strolled down the sidewalk.

9 781962 056007